A NOCTURNAL VISIT

The figure stepped away from the door, started across the room. Bolt saw the feminine shape of the nightgown, the flowing lines of the light robe, the puff of blond hair that looked gray in the dim light of the moon."

"Harmony?" he whispered.

"Quiet, Bolt," Harmony whispered.

Bolt heard the rustle of her gown as she tiptoed toward him, smelled the heady aroma of her delicate scent as she came closer. She didn't speak again until she stood next to the bed.

"I had to wait until the others were asleep."

"Is there something wrong?"

"Nothing that you can't take care of," she whispered in a low, sultry voice. She slipped the light robe from her shoulders, let it fall to the floor where it nestled in a soft heap on the braided rug. "I've been lying in bed thinking about you for more than an hour. I want you Bolt . . ."

BOLT

An Adult Western Series by Cort Martin

BOLT #21

DEADLY WITHDRAWAL

BY
CORT MARTIN

ZEBRA BOOKS
KENSINGTON PUBLISHING CORP.

ZEBRA BOOKS

are published by

Kensington Publishing Corp.
475 Park Avenue South
New York, NY 10016

First printing: November 1986

Printed in the United States of America

For Karen and Michael Madonna

A couple of city slickers who spent their honeymoon with the gunslingers at

THE ROCKING BAR RANCH

Chapter One

The sudden sound of thundering hoofbeats pounded against his ears. Startled, Jared Bolt glanced up. He saw them racing toward him and he didn't like it at all. He especially didn't like the way they were riding so fast across his land. He tensed, annoyed at the dust being kicked up by the rapidly approaching horses.

There were six riders and Bolt didn't recognize any of them. The strangers were either troublemakers who were showing off, or they were just plain rude. Either way, the sight of them set Bolt's nerves on edge. Men didn't ride that fast unless they had a reason to cover a lot of ground in a hurry. And this wasn't exactly the open prairie. This was private property. This was Bolt's ranch.

"Dammit," he muttered.

Tom Penrod, Bolt's longtime friend and partner in the cattle-raising venture, looked up. With his tousled hair and tall, lanky frame, Tom always looked like he'd just gotten out of bed. "Who in the hell are those damned fools?" he groaned.

"A heap of trouble, I reckon, judgin' from the way they're riding." Bolt shook his head.

Sweltering in the heat of the afternoon sun, Bolt and

Tom stood on the shady side of the stable with two arrogant cattle buyers who had ridden in that morning from Victoria, Texas, to purchase five hundred head of cattle. Sitting in the shade of a big oak beyond the stable were the five drovers Finch and Taylor had brought along to help them with the herd.

Maybe that was part of Bolt's irritability, too. He'd haggled with Wellington Finch and Al Taylor, the two stubborn, stuffy buyers, all day and still didn't have a firm deal. He thought if he had to listen to Finch's high, whiny voice, or look at Taylor's big, fat, obscene gut another minute, he'd grab them both by the scruff of the neck and bash their heads together. It was now late in the afternoon, and the damned picky, cigar-chewing businessmen with their fancy duds and new white felt hats wanted to inspect the cattle again, even though Bolt and Tom had already spent several hours with them out in the pasture while the buyers checked over each animal.

Bolt was offering the cattle at a fair price and he knew the buyers planned to herd the beeves back to Victoria where they could sell them for three times as much as Bolt's asking price. His patience was stretched thin and he was just about to tell the obnoxious cattle barons to go to hell when he was distracted by the approaching riders.

"Excuse me, gentlemen," Bolt said to the cattlemen. He stepped out from under the shade of the stable roof and wiped the sweat from his brow with his shirtsleeve. His irritability only increased when the lead rider of the gang of intruders skidded his horse to a halt right in front of him. A cloud of dust and loose dirt billowed up and pelted Bolt's face and clothes.

Bolt coughed and turned his head away from the choking fog. He blinked the stinging grit from his eyes, spit out a mouthful of abrasive sand. When the dust settled, he brushed the dirt from his cheeks, then glared up at the offensive stranger.

"Howdy, mister," the stranger said in a friendly voice that annoyed Bolt. The man tipped his tall, black top hat and smiled broadly down at Bolt, his white teeth stark against his dirt-smudged face. His bright red hair was short and damp, plastered flat against his head. Without the hat, the rider seemed shorter than he had first appeared.

The rank odor of the man's sweat bit at Bolt's nostrils and he tried not to breathe in the overpowering stench of damp horseflesh.

"What's your damned hurry? This is private property, in case you hadn't noticed," he snapped. He tried to brush the loose dirt off of his sweat-soaked chambray shirt, but instead only smeared it deep into the fabric.

"The name's O'Rourke," the rider said with an Irish trill to his cheerful voice. "Barney O'Rourke, and we be needin' some water for our poor, weary horses."

"I wouldn't doubt it," Bolt said with obvious sarcasm. He saw the damp, shimmering hide of O'Rourke's big black horse, the flared rubbery nostrils that seemed to gasp for air. He glanced beyond O'Rourke at the other snorting horses, which were all roan-colored and considerably smaller than the Irishman's stallion. He noticed that the rest of the riders, who stayed well behind their leader, were dark-skinned. They wore grimy, faded trousers, tattered shirts, and dark felt hats with wide, floppy brims. Mexicans, he knew. And with the heavy pistols each of them, including O'Rourke, wore in the holsters strapped to their legs, they looked like a bunch of tough outlaws. "Looks to me like you've been pushing those horses too damned hard," he commented dryly.

9

"That we have. What be your name, mister?" O'Rourke asked.

"Bolt."

"Are you the big boss of this here spread, Mr. Bolt?"

"I own this ranch. And the name's just Bolt, no mister."

"Pleased to be meetin' you, Bolt," the Irishman said as he slid his top hat back on his head and straightened the front of his shirt.

"Skip the pleasantries. What do you want?"

"My friends and I would be much obliged if we could water our horses and get a long drink of water for ourselves as well. It's been a long, hot, dusty trail."

"There's a stream at the edge of my property," Bolt said with no warmth or friendliness to his voice. He flicked his arm out straight and pointed toward the thick line of cottonwoods and tall elm trees to the south. "Good drinking water. Help yourselves." He turned and started back for the shade of the stable.

"Thank you, sir, Now there's just one more bit of hospitality we would ask of you," O'Rourke called out.

Bolt whirled to face the Irishman, the expression on his face stern, his eyes cold.

"We saw your sign out front," O'Rourke said, still beaming proudly. "We be needin' a place to stay tonight and if it wouldn't be puttin' you out none, we could use a nice hot meal, as well."

Bolt's temper flared. He felt his muscles tense, his teeth clench. Felt the flush of anger creep up his neck and color his cheeks. He wished everybody, including the two obstinate cattle buyers, would just go away and leave him alone. He looked over at Tom. Tom shook his head slightly, an expression of warning in

10

his eyes. Bolt whirled back around to face the bothersome Irishman.

"If you read the sign out front, then you know that this is the Rocking Bar Ranch and Bordello," he said as he clamped his hands to his hips and stood with his feet apart. With his lean frame and whipcord-tough, sinewy muscles showing beneath his clinging shirt, he made an impressive figure. The afternoon sun glinted off his .45 Colt, which rested in its holster at his hip. He had broken many a girl's heart with his deep blue eyes and his coal-black hair that now jutted out from under his Stetson. "It's a private ranch, stranger, and the bordello is only open at night."

"Oh, I'm sure my friends'll want to be takin' their pleasure with your fine women while we're stayin' here tonight," O'Rourke chuckled. "Of course, that'll be after they wash the trail dust off and fill their bellies with a hearty supper."

Bolt fumed at O'Rourke's exasperating gall. "We don't run a hotel here, mister. We don't rent rooms and we don't serve hot meals to drifters. San Antonio's just two miles north of here. I'm sure you and your friends can find what you're looking for in town."

"But we just rode down from thataway and we're heading on south," O'Rourke pleaded.

"Then you can just ride back up thataway," Bolt said firmly. "It's the closest town around."

"Ahh, Bolt, sir, when I read your sign out front and saw that you ran a bordello here, I figured you'd be more friendly toward strangers than most other folks. That's why we stopped here. If I've done something to offend you, I be truly sorry about it." The small Irishman sighed.

Bolt let his hands fall to his sides. "If you want to use the bordello, you're welcome to do so this evening. But we still don't run a boardinghouse here. You'll have to look elsewhere for food and lodging."

"Look, Bolt, I don't want to seem pushy, but we've been riding for four days and nights now, sleeping for only a few short stretches at a time. Fact is, we rode straight through the night last night and we all be plumb worn out, clear down to our toenails. I don't think any of us could be ridin' another inch right now. And our horses, they need to be restin' up, too. We just be wantin' a place to put our heads down and stretch out for the night." O'Rourke took a deep breath and looked down at Bolt with a sad, pleading expression in his hazel eyes.

"And what's so damned urgent that you've got to be riding day and night, O'Rourke? Who you running from? The law?"

"Ahh, by golly, Bolt, you've got me tagged all wrong." The Irishman shook his head slowly. "It be a real personal matter, you see, but it's crucial that we reach our destination as soon as possible. That's why we need to be headin' out before dawn tomorrow morning. But we just gotta get some rest first. Just a place to sleep, that's all we ask. Even if we could spread our bedrolls out on the ground, we'd be grateful. I promise you we won't be causin' you any trouble."

Bolt studied O'Rourke more closely, and as he did he felt his muscles begin to relax. The Irishman, with his small pixielike face, his slightly turned-up nose and his off-center smile, reminded Bolt of a jolly leprechaun. And there was something about O'Rourke, something about his twinkling, yet sad, expressive eyes that made Bolt want to trust him. It was a gut instinct, and Bolt was seldom wrong about such things.

Besides, Bolt made it a habit to keep his nose out of other people's affairs when it didn't involve him. He didn't know what these fellows were up to, but he believed that O'Rourke was sincere when he said that all he wanted was a place to sleep and a little food. Hell, if this bunch of strangers wanted anything else from him, they could have ridden in with pistols drawn. And since his two ranch hands, Chet and Rusty, were the only ones who lived in the big bunkhouse near the stable, Bolt didn't see any reason why he couldn't let the strangers sleep on the extra cots in there for the night.

"I'll tell you what," he said as he wiped the sweat from his brow again. "You fellows can sleep in the bunkhouse tonight. And when my two ranch hands come in from the fields and start their supper, maybe they'll toss a little extra food in the pot for all of you if you want to pay them for the trouble."

"That'd be fine with us," O'Rourke beamed with his crooked smile. "We surely appreciate your kindness and you won't be sorry you put this weary bunch of travelers up for the night."

"I'm counting on it," Bolt said as he turned and walked back over to Tom Penrod and the stubborn cattle buyers.

"They've made a decision," Tom announced.

"Yes," said Al Taylor, the one with the big gut. He flicked the ashes off of his cigar, then stuffed the wet end of it into the corner of his mouth and let it dangle as he spoke. "We'll pay your price. We're going to ride out to the pasture and round up the cattle we want so we can be on our way before it gets any later." He motioned for his drovers to join them.

"Good. Tom, will you ride out with them and see if you can give them a hand?"

"Yeah, I was planning to."

"If you can find Chet and Rusty out there, they can help you," Bolt said, wanting to get the task done in a

13

hurry and the buyers out of his hair as soon as possible. "I want to stick pretty close to the house."

"I understand," Tom said as he glanced over at the bunch of rough-looking strangers.

"I have a bank draft for you, Bolt," Taylor said as he reached inside his jacket.

"Tom can handle it when you're through rounding up the cattle."

When Bolt turned around to head up to the house, he was surprised to see that O'Rourke hadn't budged. The other five riders had gathered around their leader, but they all still sat their horses, as if they were waiting to be told what to do next.

"The bunkhouse is over there," Bolt said and pointed to the long wooden structure.

"There's just one more thing we be askin' of you," O'Rourke said with a big, broad smile.

Bolt let out a big sigh and shook his head in total frustration.

"What is it now?" he snapped. "You want me to draw your bath, or wash your dirty clothes, or polish your boots?"

"Oh, no, nothing like that," the Irishman laughed. "It be just a small request."

"You're pushing me too far, O'Rourke."

The short Irishman continued to smile. "We be needin' a place for my daughter to sleep."

Bolt's eyes widened in surprise. Then he frowned and glanced around at the other dirt-covered, gun-toting intruders. He peered into their smudged faces, looked at their faded shirts and trousers in an effort to make out any feminine characteristics.

When the rider next to Barney O'Rourke removed her hat and her long, dark hair tumbled free of its trappings, Bolt was astonished. He looked again and saw no traces of swollen breasts or feminine curves

14

beneath her loose-fitting shirt and trousers.

"This here's my daughter, Lupita," the Irishman said, with obvious pride in his voice. "Lupita O'Rourke. Ain't she purty?"

The girl smiled shyly at Bolt, and, for a long moment, stared directly at him with dark, searching eyes, as if she were trying to read him mind. As if her very life depended on his reaction to her.

Bolt was caught off guard by the girl's disarming smile, by her penetrating gaze. He dared not lower his eyes again in search of mounded breasts. Not only was he surprised to see a girl in men's clothing, but he was even more astonished to learn that this dark-complexioned girl was O'Rourke's daughter. Obviously, she had Spanish or Mexican blood in her. A mestiza.

He knew he was staring, but he couldn't take his eyes off her. Her face was small and pixielike, like her father's and he saw that she had the same turned-up nose, the same expressive eyes, except that hers were dark instead of hazel.

"Pleased to meet you," Bolt finally said awkwardly.

Lupita smiled again and he saw that her smile was off-center, just like her father's.

"Have you got a place where Lupita can sleep tonight?" asked O'Rourke. "It ain't right for her to be sleepin' in the bunkhouse with all these fellows."

"Uh, uh, yes," Bolt stammered, relieved to look away from the girl's magnetic gaze. "She can sleep in the bordello with the other girls."

"Now just a damned minute, Bolt," O'Rourke said. "My Lupita is a good girl. She ain't gonna be sleepin' in no bordello with a bunch of whores."

"The harlots who work for me are good girls, too, O'Rourke," Bolt said, his voice suddenly cold again. "And there's plenty of room upstairs. Your daughter can have a bedroom to herself."

"No, sir," O'Rourke protested. "I don't want my Lupita even associating with that kind of woman. Why, she's just barely eighteen years old, no more than a child. I'll guarantee that she's still an innocent little girl and I don't want her seeing or hearing anything that might offend her."

"Father, please," Lupita said as she lowered her head in embarrassment.

"There's nothing to worry about," Bolt said. "The girls use the little cottages behind the bordello to, uh, ply their trade. The big building that we call the bordello is nothing more than a place to meet the customers. It's a house with a large living room across the front and a bedroom and kitchen in the back. The girls sleep in the bedrooms upstairs, but they don't work there."

"No, I won't hear of it," O'Rourke said. "Lupita will not sleep in that . . . that house."

"It's up to you, O'Rourke," Bolt shrugged. "She either sleeps in the bordello or she sleeps in the bunkhouse with all the men. Unless you want her to sleep outside on the ground someplace."

"What about that house right back up there on the hill?" O'Rourke nodded. "Couldn't she sleep up there?"

"That's my house. That's where I sleep," Bolt told O'Rourke. He resented the Irishman's even suggesting such a thing. That was his house, his haven, and he didn't want anyone invading his privacy. He glanced over at the mestiza, hoping she hadn't taken offense at his refusal to allow her to sleep in his house. It was then that he suddenly realized how pretty she was, with her dark, expressive eyes, her long, black, flowing hair that shone in the sunlight like a crow's wing. Even with her face smudged with dirt, she was

16

pretty. Even in those awful, baggy men's clothes that gave her no shape. "I think your daughter would be better off sleeping with the girls."

Lupita's head jerked up and she stared hard at Bolt. A puzzled expression creased her face as her dark eyes searched his. It was as if she were looking for some secret meaning to his words. Then she smiled coyly and settled back against her saddle, as if she'd figured him out. She continued to stare at him, and the playful expression in her dark eyes unnerved him.

Bolt wondered if she was flirting with him. He'd seen that hungry, teasing look in a young woman's eyes before, and he figured she was indeed flirting with him.

A sudden warmth flooded his body, a warmth that came from within instead of from the intense heat of the day. He felt stifled, dry of mouth. He sensed the sparks that flew between then as they studied each other like skulking cats. He wondered what she was thinking. He wondered why she was riding with this rough-looking bunch of men. He noticed the small carpetbag that was tied to the back of her saddle and wondered what she carried in it. He wondered so many things about her.

Barney O'Rourke's voice brought Bolt out of his reverie.

"I think maybe you be right, Bolt," the Irishman said. "I think my Lupita would be better off sleeping with your girls."

Bolt turned his head and looked at O'Rourke. He knew by the stern look on the Irishman's face that O'Rourke had seen him staring at Lupita.

"Yes," Bolt agreed. "Your daughter will have the privacy of her own room in the bordello and she won't be bothered by anyone." He wondered why he couldn't speak her name, why his tongue seemed tied

17

in knots when he tried. Lupita. It was a pretty name, a fitting name for such a pretty young woman. He cleared his throat, cleared his mind of the thoughts that kept intruding on him. "I'm sure she'll be quite comfortable there and I know my girls will take good care of your daughter."

Although he tried not to, he looked at Lupita again.

Her eyes flickered playfully when she smiled coyly at him. Yes, she was flirting. He was sure of it.

She knew.

Bolt took a deep breath and let it out slowly.

That bunch of gun-toting intruders might be troublemakers, but Bolt had the feeling that it was Lupita O'Rourke who would cause him the most trouble.

Chapter Two

"I still say you made a mistake letting them hard-cases stay here tonight," Tom Penrod said. "You know damn well they're up to no good."

"They'll be gone before dawn," Bolt said. "Quit worrying about it."

Bolt and Tom stood on the back porch of the big ranch house, enjoying the cool night air and an after-dinner smoke while they discussed the events of the day. Tom had told Bolt about the final irritations he'd had with the arrogant cattle buyers, Finch and Taylor, before the two men had finally rounded up the cattle and herded them away. A few minutes ago, as they watched the Irishman and his four Mexican companions stroll from the bunkhouse over to the bordello, their conversation had drifted into the subject of the strangers who'd ridden in that afternoon.

Harmony Sanchez, the pretty young blonde who did all of their cooking and cleaning, had already walked down the lamplit path to the bordello where she would spend the evening all gussied up in a long, fancy gown. She served as the madam for Bolt's bordello and enjoyed her job of greeting the customers and serving them drinks. But she was more than that. She was a friend to the harlots, a mother hen to them, although at twenty-two she was only a couple of years older than the four girls. Harmony slept in the downstairs bedroom at the bordello, except for those special nights when she came to Bolt's bed.

Bolt adored Harmony, and one of the things he liked best about her was that she realized that he wasn't ready to settle down with a wife and family. They'd already gone through the times when she was jealous and possessive of him, and although she still constantly teased him about his other women, she was now independent enough to be happy being his helpmate and his occasional bed partner. Harmony came to him when she had her needs, but she also had the ability to sense when he needed her.

"A lot could happen between now and dawn," Tom said dryly. "I don't trust a damned one of them."

"Tom, you worry too much. Why don't you ride into town and find yourself a nice warm body to climb."

"Not tonight, Bolt. If trouble breaks out, and I'll bet my last dollar that it will, you're gonna need all the help you can get."

Bolt wasn't paying much attention to his friend just then. He was concentrating on the girl who had just stepped out onto the front porch of the bordello below them. The girl was dressed in a long, flowing gown that shimmered in the soft light of the porch lanterns, and at first Bolt thought it was one of his harlots. He squinted his eyes, and when he saw her long, dark hair he realized that the girl was Lupita O'Rourke.

It surprised him to see the mestiza in a dress. In the glow of the lamplight he saw the outline of her breasts, her small waistline. She looked much more feminine than he'd imagined she would be, and he felt the flush of excitement course through his loins.

He wondered if the gown was one of her own or

whether she'd borrowed it from one of the harlots. He knew she'd brought a carpetbag with her, so it was likely that she carried clothes other than the baggy shirt and trousers that she'd been wearing when she and the other strangers had ridden onto his ranch earlier that day.

He wondered why a young, pretty girl like Lupita was riding with her father and the Mexicans who looked like outlaws. The rugged trail was certainly no place for a lady. Most women didn't travel at all, and those who did usually rode in a stagecoach. He wondered where the strangers were headed, and why they were in such a hurry. It didn't really matter. They'd be gone before dawn and he'd probably never see them again.

"Bolt, are you listening to me?" Tom said.

"Yeah, what'd you say?"

"I thought so. Dammit, Bolt, I wish you hadn't let those outlaws stay here."

"You don't know that they're outlaws. And even if they are, so what? They wanted a place to sleep and I gave it to them. You seem to forget that you and I rode the owlhoot trail a few years back."

"But we weren't outlaws."

"No, but until we proved our innocence, there were a few lawmen and a whole bunch of bounty hunters who thought we were. And it hasn't been so long ago that I've forgotten how grateful we were when we had a soft bed to sleep on instead of the hard ground."

"Well, if we make it through the night without trouble, I'll be be surprised." Tom muttered.

Bolt took a deep drag from his cigarette, tossed it down to the wooden planks of the porch, and stomped it out with his boot. He blew the smoke out slowly as he looked down at Lupita again.

"Come on, Tom, let's go on down and see what's happening."

It took only a few minutes for Bolt and Tom to make their way down the hill. The path was lit by several hurricane lanterns that hung from posts. Off to their left, Bolt saw the glow from the bunkhouse lamps as it spilled through the windows, and outside the nearby stable a lantern shone down on O'Rourke's black stallion and the five roan horses that were tied up to the hitching rail.

As they were walking down the hill the sound of a familiar tune being plinked out on the piano keys started up and floated out on the night air. That was a good sign. Harmony wouldn't be playing the piano if there was any hint of trouble inside the bordello.

"Hear that music?" Bolt said.

"Yeah, I hear it," Tom grumbled.

"Everything's fine."

"So far, maybe."

Their boots clanked against the wooden steps as they walked up to the porch of the bordello. Bolt's heart fluttered when he glanced over at Lupita who stood at the railing like some elegant goddess. When she turned her head and smiled, something melted deep inside Bolt. He nodded and headed toward her.

"I'll go on inside," Tom said as he walked through the open door of the bordello.

The piano music stopped and was replaced by the sound of conversation, laughter.

"Good evening, Miss O'Rourke," Bolt said as he tipped his hat. "I hope you've had a chance to rest."

"Yes, thank you, Mr. Bolt. Your girls have been very kind to me."

Lupita's voice was musical, with its mixture of a Spanish accent and an Irish brogue. Her scent floated on the evening breeze and filled Bolt's nostrils. She smelled fresh and clean, like fresh-picked lavender and new-mown grass.

"Did you get enough to eat?"

"Oh, yes," she laughed. "The girls are good cooks and I'm afraid I ate too much. I just wanted to get some fresh air before I go to bed." She stared out into the darkness and took a deep breath.

Bolt took a deep breath, too, but it was because he was studying her profile. He saw the streaks of gold that shimmered through her long, dark, shiny hair as it caught the flickering light of the porch lamp. Her dress, with its high neckline and full skirt, was simple, but it showed her figure off to advantage. The dress was dark blue, and when it caught the same golden light of the lamp, it looked like it was a royal gown of purple.

He stepped over beside her and leaned against the rail, stared out into the night.

"Does it bother you that your father's in there?" He nodded toward the bordello.

"Oh, no," she smiled as she turned her head to look at him. "He's just having a drink before he goes back over to the bunkhouse to go to bed."

"I reckon so."

"That's all he's doing, Mr. Bolt," she said firmly. "My father isn't the kind who would use the services of a prostitute."

"All sorts of men visit bordellos, Miss O'Rourke. Bachelors, lonely men, happily married men, fellows who ride the trail. You get a few bad apples sometimes, but most of the men who pay for a woman's pleasure are decent folks. There's really nothing wrong with it."

"Maybe so, but my father wouldn't cheat on my

mother. He loves her too much."

"Your mother's still alive, then?"

Bolt thought he saw a sadness in her eyes before she turned to stare out into the darkness again, but he couldn't be sure.

"Yes, she's alive. Why do you ask?"

"No reason, really. I just thought it strange that you were riding the rugged trail with your father and those other fellows. I figured maybe there was nobody at home to take care of you."

"I ride with my father by choice, Mr. Bolt, and in case you hadn't noticed, I'm old enough to take care of myself."

Bolt had noticed, but he didn't say so. He shifted positions, turned sideways to face her.

"Are you on your way home?" he asked.

"You ask a lot of questions, Mr. Bolt."

"I don't mean anything by it. I just wondered where you were headed."

"As my father told you earlier, Mr. Bolt, it's a personal matter, and quite frankly, none of your business." She tilted her head up proudly.

He saw her dark eyes flash with anger and wondered what the big mystery was about. He admired her for her spunk, but was also annoyed by it.

"I didn't mean to pry, but riding the way you are, pushing so hard, can wear a person out. You really looked tired when you rode in today, and I'm just concerned about you."

"I thank you for that, Mr. Bolt, but I'd rather not talk about it."

There was a long, awkward silence as they both stared up at the star-studded sky. The moon, which was still low in the sky, looked like someone had sliced off the lower part of it. It would be a few more nights before it was full. He listened to the hum of the frogs down by the river, heard the constant thrum of the crickets in the fields.

"Your mother must be a very pretty lady," he said finally, trying to ease the tension between them.

"Yes, she is. She's Mexican, as I'm sure you've figured out. I'm a half-breed."

"A pretty one, I might say."

"Why, Mr. Bolt, are you flirting with me?" she teased.

He smiled, glad that she wasn't mad at him.

"Do you want me to flirt with you, Miss O'Rourke?"

"Please call me Lupita," she said, not answering his question.

"Only if you drop the 'mister' and call me Bolt. You're proud of your mother, aren't you?"

"Of course, I am. I'm proud of both of my parents. Aren't you proud of yours?"

"My father's a minister and I have a lot of respect for him. Yes, I reckon I'm proud of him, although I'd never thought about it that way."

"He's a minister, and you run a bordello? What does he think of that?"

"He's the one who taught me to live and let live. I wish I had a penny for every time he preached about the virtues of doing what you felt was right as long as you didn't hurt anyone else."

"What about your mother?"

"She's dead."

"Oh, I'm sorry."

"No need to be. She died when I was a young boy. I don't even remember her."

"That's sad, not to remember your own mother."

Lupita lowered her head and put her hand to her

mouth, as if she were about to cry. She seemed lost in her own thoughts.

"It's sad, but my father told me all about her, and I know she was a good woman."

"Bolt, what's it like to be a harlot?" Lupita asked, changing the subject abruptly.

Bolt couldn't figure her out. She changed moods quicker than any woman he'd ever known. One minute she was cheerful, playful, and the next, she was angry or melancholy. But she had a mind of her own and she didn't mind expressing her thoughts.

"I don't know," Bolt laughed. "I guess you'd have to ask one of the harlots."

"You know, they seem like such nice girls. So normal. They were very kind to me."

"They are nice girls, all of them."

"They think a lot of you, too," Lupita smiled. "They tell me you're a pretty decent man."

"You don't believe them, do you?" he laughed.

"I don't know," she teased. "I haven't made up my mind yet."

Bolt heard the sound of hard-riding horses off in the distance. That was one of the things he liked about living out in the country, on the open prairie with its rolling hills. He could hear the horses out on the road. He could hear them approaching long before they reached his property and knew from which direction they came. And he could always tell when they slowed and turned off at his ranch.

He cocked his head and listened. Lupita heard them, too, and turned her head in that direction.

Above the sound of the crickets and frogs, the din from the bordello, he heard the fast-approaching horses slow as the sound of the hoofbeats changed from a thundering, pounding vibration to a scuffling, shuffling noise. The horses were coming down his private road, riding past his house. But this didn't surprise Bolt. This was the time of evening when the bordello always got busy. It was the time of night when neighboring ranch hands came to the bordello after a hard day's work. When businessmen, townsmen, and other lonely fellows rode in from San Antonio to satisfy their needs.

The thing that surprised him was that there were so many horses coming at once. Six or seven, at least. Maybe more. Usually the customers drifted in one at a time, or in pairs. This was a Monday night, and on most Monday evenings, for some reason Bolt didn't understand, there usually weren't enough customers to keep the four harlots busy.

He heard the horses slow even more as they neared the bunkhouse and stable. He saw their dark outlines when they came into view, and he quickly counted eight riders.

"Looks like it's going to be a busy night," he commented.

"I'd better go on inside now," Lupita told him.

"Why?" Bolt asked, not wanting her to leave him. "The men are coming to visit the girls."

"I certainly don't want those fellows to think that I'm one of the harlots," she giggled.

"I understand," Bolt laughed. "I've enjoyed talking to you."

Lupita offered her hand and Bolt took it in his, felt the warmth of it, the soft smoothness.

"It's been my pleasure, Bolt. Thank you for your hospitality."

"You're welcome here anytime, Lupita."

"I guess I won't be seeing you again, Bolt."

She squeezed his hand and he detected the sadness

27

in her voice, saw it in her dark eyes.

"Don't be too sure about that," he grinned. "It would be worth it to get up before dawn, just to see your pretty face again."

"Why, Mr. Bolt, you are flirting with me," she giggled. "Goodnight, sir."

She withdrew her hand, rose up on tiptoes, and gave him a quick kiss on the cheek. She turned and quickly went inside the bordello.

After she was gone, Bolt could still feel the warmth of her smooth hand in his, could feel the tingling brush of her soft lips against his cheek.

"Well, I see the lady's taken a fancy to you," Tom Penrod said as he stepped out onto the porch.

"Does that surprise you, Tom?" Bolt grinned.

Tom walked over to Bolt and glanced down at the new arrivals. "Looks like the gals are gonna earn their money tonight."

"They earn it every night, Tom."

"Yeah, I know. So far, those damned outlaws are behaving themselves."

"I hate to say I told you so, and we don't know that they're outlaws, so quit calling them that."

Bolt turned around and watched the eight riders dismount and stretch their legs before they tied their horses to the long hitching rail. The men walked over and gathered at the foot of the steps.

"Good evening, gentlemen," Bolt called down from the top of the steps. "Come on up. We're open, but you may have to wait your turn."

The men just stood there.

"Do either of you fellows own one of those roan horses over by the stable? Or that big black stallion?" the short, heavy-set man in the middle asked.

"No," said Bolt.

"Who do they belong to?"

"Who's asking?"

"I'm Sheriff Ben Cotter, from Austin, Texas," the pudgy man said as he flashed his tin badge. "And the owners of those horses robbed the Austin Territorial Bank four days ago."

Tom jabbed Bolt in the side with his elbow. "I hate to say I told you so," he whispered gleefully.

"Shut up Tom. Are you sure about that, sheriff?" Bolt called out. A sickness settled into his stomach when he thought about Lupita. She knew. She was a part of this, the deceitful little hussy.

"Damned sure," the sheriff said in a loud, deep voice. "What's your name, mister?"

"It's Bolt."

"And what are you doing here?"

"I own this ranch. My partner here and I own it."

"What's your partner's name?"

"It's Penrod," Tom answered.

"Where are the other horses?" Sheriff Cotter demanded.

"What other horses?" Bolt asked.

"I was expectin' to find eight horses. There were eight bandits who robbed that Austin bank."

"I don't know anything about that," Bolt said.

"If that's the way you want to be, fine with me," the sheriff said, "but I'm placing you under arrest for the bank robbery in Austin. Both of you."

"The hell you are," Bolt shouted. "We had nothing to do with any holdup."

"You masterminded the robbery, Bolt. We've been tracking those men for four days now and it appears they came straight to your ranch. It doesn't take much to figure it out."

"I told you, sheriff, I don't know anything about

29

your stinking little bank holdup."

"It's not a little holdup. The bastards got away with fifty thousand dollars and they killed two innocent people in the process. Murdered them in cold blood. The bank teller and an innocent woman who happened to be at the bank on business."

"I'm sorry about all that, sheriff, but don't blame me for your troubles."

"I am blaming you, Bolt. You masterminded the whole damned thing and you're gonna pay for it."

Sheriff Ben Cotter reached for his pistol.

Chapter Three

Bolt's muscles tautened. His nerves felt like a thousand tightly wound coils ready to spring. He watched all of the men of the posse, but his attention was drawn to Sheriff Cotter, whose hand rested on his holster. He wore his holster too high on his hip to get an easy draw, and the way his hand was poised, with his wrist bent straight down, he looked like he was pointing to the weapon instead of preparing to draw it.

The corpulent lawman had a bearing about him that irritated Bolt. Cotter stood with his short legs spread apart, his feet planted firmly on the ground, in an authoritative stance. His big belly jutted out like an overgrown watermelon. His left hand clutched the fabric of his shirt, the thumb hooked around the material in a manner that pushed his star-shaped badge out so that it was prominently displayed. The gold rope braid on his stiff hat matched the epaulet braid on his shoulders and made him look like some high-powered general.

"I didn't mastermind shit!" Bolt yelled down from the porch of the bordello.

"Then how come the bandits headed straight for your place?" Cotter wanted to know.

"I can't tell you that, sheriff."

"You mean you won't tell me that." Sheriff Cotter's deep, raspy voice boomed out in the night. "You planned the whole damned robbery, you low-down skunk of a bastard. I know you did. Those stinkin' yellow-bellied thieves ran off with more'n fifty thousand greenbacks. What's your slice of the cheese, Bolt? Half? Did you get twenty-five thousand just for ten minutes' work in planning it? Pretty fair wages, if you ask me."

"I told you I don't know anything about any damned robbery."

"Yair. I see you for what you are, Bolt, a low-down, stinkin' skunk of a bastard who runs a filthy whorehouse. I know your type. And I know you ramrodded that bank robbery in Austin."

"You don't know horseshit, sheriff," Bolt roared. "You wear your brains in your shoes."

Their loud, shouting voices exploded on the night air as the heated argument continued. Tom Penrod stood near his friend, a half-smile on his face, thoroughly enjoying the exchange.

"You're talkin' to the law, mister. You'd better watch your filthy mouth."

"You ain't no different from those damned bandits, Cotter. You're just standin' on a different side of the fence, that's all."

"Yair, well, you're on the wrong side of the fence, Bolt. You shouldn't have become so friendly with them pigsuckin' swine."

"I don't know 'em, sheriff, and I certainly ain't friendly with 'em. Hell, I don't even know their goddamned names."

"Then how come the bandits' horses are hitched up outside your stable right now? How come the thievin' bastards made a beeline for your ranch right after the robbery? Explain that one, if you can."

"The men who rode in on those horses are strangers. I swear it. They asked for a place to stay tonight and I told them they could sleep in the bunkhouse. A few hours' rest. That's all they wanted from me."

"Is that where they are now?" Sheriff Cotter turned his head briefly to glance at the lights of the bunkhouse. "Did robbing the bank wear them out? Are they over there catchin' up on their sleep?"

"None of your damned business, sheriff."

"So you're refusin' to cooperate with the law. Have it your way, then." Cotter stood up tall, stuck out his chest. "So be it. In addition to arresting you for conspiracy in connection with the robbery, Mr. Bolt, I hereby place you under arrest for harboring fugitives. And if you continue to refuse to answer my questions, I'll add a few more charges to the list. Enough of 'em to keep you behind bars until you rot."

Bolt fumed. "I told you what I know. They're strangers who just happened to stop at my ranch to seek shelter for the night. I gave them a place to sleep. That doesn't make me a goddamned criminal."

"But hiding them out does," Cotter smirked.

"I'm not hiding anybody out, dammit. I don't know these men, I tell you. When they came here and asked for a place to bed down, I didn't know they'd robbed a bank, for chrissakes. I never saw 'em before."

"What do you do here, run a haven for outlaws?" the sheriff accused. "Yair, it makes sense. That's why you have that filthy whorehouse here. I thought it was kind of peculiar to find a house full of whores so far out here in the sticks, but now I understand."

"I run a cattle ranch here," Bolt said, his voice hard, firm. "An honest, hard-working cattle ranch. I got no time to entertain hardcases."

"Makes a nice cover for hiding outlaws, doesn't it?" Cotter taunted.

"They're strangers, dammit."

"And you weren't suspicious of them?" Cotter snapped. "You really expect me to believe that?"

"Believe what you want to, sheriff. I didn't do anything wrong."

"You're telling me you don't question strangers before you open your house to them and put 'em up for the night?"

"I don't question anyone unless they're bothering me. And speaking of that, you're a long ways south of your jurisdiction, aren't you, sheriff?"

"Don't get smart with me, Bolt. If you're not hiding them bandits out, then I'm sure you won't mind telling me where they are. Are they in there, stuffing their limp noodles into your filthy whores?" Cotter nodded toward the bordello.

"Yeah, they're in there."

"Step aside," Cotter ordered as he motioned his men to follow him.

"Just a damned minute," Bolt yelled. "You can't go in there."

Bolt dashed down the steps to block the way of the sheriff and his posse. His hand streaked to his holster and hovered just above the butt of his pistol. Tom followed him down the stairs and took up a position beside his friend, made ready to draw.

"Me and my deputies are going in after those bandits and you'd better not try to stop us. You give me any trouble, Bolt, and I'll tack another charge onto the list. I'll get you for obstructing justice," Cotter bellowed as he whipped his pistol out.

The sheriff's deputies drew their weapons and prepared to storm the bordello.

"Not until I get the women out of there. They have

34

nothing to do with the crime that's been committed, and I ain't gonna let you go in until they're safely out. You can wait that long," Bolt insisted. He snagged his pistol out of its holster, aimed it at Cotter's gut in an attempt to hold the determined posse at bay so he could get Lupita, Harmony, and the four harlots out of the building before the bullets started to fly.

In the next instant, he realized that he was already too late to stop the horror of a gun battle.

He heard the shattering tinkle of breaking glass. Before he could move, a shot rang out from upstairs. A deputy clawed at his gut and staggered sideways, blood oozing from a hole just below his beltline. He coughed and pitched forward in a slump. His pistol tumbled from his hand and danced, cartwheeled into the dust.

For one brief instant, a ghostly silence fell over the dark, shadowy land as the stunned lawmen froze, recovered from the shock of the explosion, and glanced around, their hands clutching loaded pistols, their eyes darting from here to there, frantically searching for the gunman.

Then, all kinds of hell broke loose.

Three Mexican outlaws burst through the door of the bordello, sixguns blazing. Two of them wore only white undershorts, the third one wore shorts and an open shirt that had been grabbed up in his hurry. Barney O'Rourke, fully clothed, followed on their heels, his pistol bucking in his hand.

Explosions punched holes in the silence and fire belched from a half-dozen weapons. White smoke billowed from gun barrels and men shouted and yelled warnings like sailors on a sinking ship. A man screamed as a stray bullet thocked into his flesh.

Bullets flew from both directions as Bolt and Tom were caught in the crossfire.

Bolt went into a crouch and hunkered down as he drove a zigzag path away from the bordello, the sheriff, and his deputies. Guns bucked and barked and the air sizzled with flying lead, but he knew he could catch a ball if he stayed near the lawmen.

Tom ducked down low and backed away from the porch just in time to keep from getting trampled by the rush of outlaws who shot their way down the steps and dashed into the fray, disappearing in the layer of smoke that hung over the bloody battlefield.

Cotter stood there like a statue, taking aim, hammering back and triggering while his men scattered like flushed quail and shot blindly at smoke and muzzle flashes.

Bolt saw a shadow framed by bronze lamplight cross a window and he fired instinctively, knowing it was a man by the hat, the bulk of shoulders. He heard a muffled cry, saw the curtains rustle like smoke, flutter like a grandmother's dreary shawl. He saw the man stiffen, totter, and fade away as he fell backward away from the window. Bolt's eyes held steady as the lamplight flickered from the crash of the body on the hardwood floor.

Bolt's attention was drawn back down to the front of the bordello, to Lupita O'Rourke standing in the doorway.

"Get back, Lupita," he shouted, and saw the girl duck back inside the building.

"Kill 'em boys!" shouted Cotter. "Kill ever' damn one of 'em."

Bolt nearly retched to hear the slavering voice of the sheriff, who seemed bent on killing, no matter the danger to the innocent women inside the bordello.

A rifle shot broke eardrums, and a deputy's face disappeared in a cloud of blood. He went down like a man hammered with a sixteen-pound maul, and his

36

body twitched like a gigged frog as his reflexes continued to function long after his brain had been blown into crimson mush. Bolt turned away, sick to his stomach, sick in his mind at this brainless slaughter of good men bent on blind justice.

One of O'Rourke's men burst through the front doors, sixguns in both fists. Bolt saw the wide stain of crimson on the outlaw's shirt and knew he was the man who'd been upstairs in the window only a minute before.

The wounded outlaw dropped one man and sent another one diving for the ground. Bolt and Cotter both opened up and laced the Mexican outlaw dead with bullets that dissected his lungs. His legs wobbled for a moment, then collapsed and he crumpled into a dead heap on the porch.

The smoke stung Bolt's lungs and blinded him, clogged his nostrils. Pistol fire sounded like giant boulders striking tin roofs, metal barrels. The roar was deafening, and no one could see through the thick drapes of white smoke that cottoned the battleground like batting.

Bolt heard a bullet strike bone and he saw another deputy wobble toward him on dying legs, his mouth opened to scream, but his eyes wide with the awful fear of death and his face whiter than the smoke, whiter than the eternal clouds that floated over timeless graveyards.

"Jesus," Bolt muttered, as the man, not yet thirty by his looks, fell headlong onto the ground in front of him, his blood soaking into the dry ground and pooling up into a miniature lake. The young man looked up at Bolt and stretched out a trembling arm. His mouth worked, but no sound passed his lips. He blinked once, looked up a thousand yards into the black night sky, and shuddered in the final throes of

37

death.

Lupita appeared briefly at the doorway again.

"Stop, Papa, before you get killed!" she shouted, then disappeared into the house.

Bolt moved, then, dashed to the corner of the porch, away from the biting smoke. He coughed, cleared his head. He saw Tom on the opposite side, his sixgun smoking. Penrod's face beamed in the flash of gunfire, and it was creased with a frown, his jaws set firm with determination. His hat was gone and his hair looked like the wind had found a place to make a small hurricane.

"Look out!" shouted Bolt as a man clad in shorts plunged from the darkness to land just behind Tom.

Penrod whirled, and Bolt saw his back and shoulders buck with the shot from Tom's pistol. The outlaw went down like a poleaxed steer, and Tom turned around, nodded his thanks to Bolt.

O'Rourke appeared out of the thick cloud of white smoke as he made a dash for the house. His body bucked as he took a bullet in the back. Bolt saw the Irish outlaw stagger and crumple to the ground. The outlaw leader groaned as he lay at the foot of the steps, his pistol still clutched in his fist. A widening circle of blood stained the ground around him.

Bolt stared at the wounded Irishman and aimed his pistol, wanting to finish him off. But he saved his bullet and kicked the pistol out of O'Rourke's hand instead, knowing that the outlaw leader wouldn't last long.

It seemed like hours. But Bolt knew that only seconds had passed by, minutes, perhaps. The gunfire faded as quickly as it had erupted.

Cotter banged off one last shot, but there was no answering salvo.

"Goddamn, we got 'em all," crowed the elated

sheriff as he stood with his arms tossed high in victory.

Bolt stood there as the smoke cleared and the silence deepened.

"Maybe," he said quietly, thinking aloud. There'd been no way for Bolt to keep count in the confusion of the smoke-filled gunfight, but if he were the sheriff, he sure as hell wouldn't be so cocky about it. He'd be watching his backside instead of standing there like some goddamned target.

"Christ, Jared, you saved my ass," said Penrod, coming up to Bolt, grinning like a shit-eating dog. He threw an arm around Jared's shoulder.

"Maybe that'll teach you to watch your backside," Bolt muttered as he peered into the darkness, not trusting the stillness that had settled over the land.

"Hell, we put out their damned lamps, didn't we?" Tom beamed.

"Don't make it sound like a damned pie supper, Tom. A lot of blood was spilled out there."

"I didn't plan the fuckin' shootout. They opened up on us."

"I wonder if the girls are all right," said Bolt, pushing empty shells from the cylinder of his pistol with the ramrod. He loaded quickly, stared up at the front of the bordello. Before he could move toward the building, Lupita appeared in the doorway.

She took a few tentative steps out to the middle of the porch, quickly scanned the battleground. She spotted her father and dashed down the steps. For an instant she stood perfectly still, staring down at him, her eyes wide with horror.

"Papa! Papa! Oh, you're still alive!" she cried as she kneeled down beside him.

"Your father won't live, girl," Sheriff Cotter called as he started toward the porch. "The stinkin' thief got

39

what he deserved, ma'am, just like all them other bandits."

"You had no right to kill him, you filthy swine," Lupita shouted at the sheriff.

"It was my duty, girl," Cotter called from ten feet away.

Bolt froze. He saw a flash of white just beyond the sheriff and knew instantly that one of the outlaws had survived the battle. One of the outlaws who wore only his undershorts. He raised his pistol, couldn't find a target in the darkness.

A shot rang out, loud and crisp in the still air.

Bolt saw the puff of white smoke behind the sheriff, saw the lawman jerk, stumble, and collapse to the ground. He heard Cotter's scream rise, then fade away.

Bolt's pistol wavered as he tried to track the outlaw, but he saw only the smoke. He peered into the dark, glanced back over his shoulder. When he turned back, he saw the outlaw standing over O'Rourke and Lupita.

"Pedro, help me!" Lupita pleaded as she jumped up from the ground.

Bolt took careful aim at the man in shorts. But he couldn't risk shooting. Not with Lupita so close.

"Give it up," Bolt called, his gun trained on the Mexican's chest.

The outlaw jerked his head, staring at Bolt for only a brief instant before he turned and fled.

Still Bolt couldn't get a round off. Damn. If Lupita had just stayed down, the Mexican would have been an easy shot.

He gave chase and saw the bandit disappear around the corner of the bordello.

"Check the house, Tom!" he shouted. "He might try to come in the back door and take the girls

40

hostage."

As Tom dashed into the bordello, Bolt rushed around to the back. He stopped, listened, then fired at the rustling of brush in the distance. He listened again, heard no scream or groan, heard no thud of a body hitting the ground and knew the outlaw had gotten away. Disappointed and angry at himself for letting the outlaw escape, he walked back around to the front of the house where Lupita was huddled over her dying father.

"Papa, please don't die!" Lupita pleaded. "We need you. We love you. Please."

"Don't tell . . . don't tell them . . . where it . . . is," O'Rourke stammered, his voice weak. "Remember . . . your mother."

"Yes, Papa, I promise."

"I love . . . you . . . Lupi. . . ." His voice trailed off as his head fell to the side.

"I love you, too, Papa," Lupita whispered as the tears welled up in her eyes.

Chapter Four

The light from the porch lanterns washed across the bloody battlefield, outlined the dark shapes of the dozen dead bodies that lay in awkward, twisted positions on the ground. Bolt stood in the middle of the carnage and shook his head.

That same soft light spilled across Lupita O'Rourke's back as she kneeled over her dead father. The moon was still low in the sky, but it had risen far enough above the row of trees to shine on Lupita's face and add silver highlights to her black hair.

Tom Penrod stood off to the side, talking quietly to the two ranch hands, Chet and Rusty, who had dashed out of the bunkhouse when the gunfire started and then just stood there, not knowing whom to shoot at.

Harmony Sanchez stood on the porch, her hands clasped over her mouth as she stared down in horror. And, behind her, the four frightened harlots talked nervously to each other in soft, low murmurs.

"Oh, no, Father. No," Lupita cried in a hushed voice as she stared down at her father's lifeless face. "Why did you do it? Why?" She leaned over and gently pushed the eyelids closed, then ran her fingers across her father's cheeks, gave him a quick kiss on the forehead.

From a few feet away, Bolt watched the mestiza. As she raised her head and stared up at the sky, as if saying a silent prayer, the moonlight shimmered into the pool of tears that gathered in her eyes. She blinked her eyes once, and Bolt saw the tears spill over the brim and trickle down her cheeks.

He was torn by his confused emotions for Lupita. He wanted so much to go over and put his hand on her shoulder, tell her that he understood, comfort her, hold her in his arms until her grief was gone. And yet, he wasn't sure that the mestiza needed, or even wanted, his comforting touch, and that bothered him, too. Lupita hadn't become hysterical about her father's death, or cried or carried on, as most girls would have, but had accepted it, her few brief tears the only sign of her grief. Even in the face of her father's death, Lupita seemed strong and courageous, and Bolt admired her for those traits.

On the other hand, Bolt was madder than hell at her. He detested her for what she'd done. And what had she actually done, he wondered, to make him so infuriated? Flirted with him? Teased him with her eyes, her coy smile? Made a fool out of him? For one thing, she'd misrepresented herself and made her father out to be a decent, innocent, happily married man who loved his wife so much that he wouldn't think of using the services of a harlot.

He now knew that Lupita was part of a ruthless bank robbery, and that she was at least partly responsible for the murders of the Austin bank teller and the innocent woman customer who had happened to be at the wrong place at the wrong time. If Lupita hadn't actually participated in the robbery, it was obvious to him that she knew about it, even condoned it, proba-

43

bly. Otherwise, why would she be riding with the robbers?

Harmony came down the steps and stood beside him. She grabbed his arm, squeezed hard, then let it go. She didn't have to say anything to let Bolt know she understood and that she was there to help if she could.

Bolt stared down at the dark ground for a minute, trying to sort out his feelings. When he saw Lupita stand up and brush the dust from the skirt of her long blue dress, he strolled over to her.

"I'm sorry about your father," he said, trying to keep the tightness in his throat from showing.

"Thank you," she said simply. She held her head high. Not smugly, but proudly, Bolt thought.

"Would you mind telling me what your father meant when he said, 'Don't tell them where it is'?" Bolt asked bluntly. "Was he talking about the money from the bank robbery?"

"I don't want to talk about it," Lupita said, with no emotion to her voice.

"What'd he mean about remembering your mother? Where is she?"

"I don't want to talk about it," she said again.

"If you know where that money is, Miss O'Rourke, you'd better talk about it."

"This is hardly the time to discuss such things, Mr. Bolt," she said as she glared at him. "My father has just died. Have you no feelings?"

"Apparently you're the one with no feelings, Miss O'Rourke," Bolt said sarcastically. "Two innocent people are dead because of your father and his friends, and I'm sure you're not concerned about them or their families. If you know where that money from the bank robbery is and don't speak up, then

44

you're just as guilty as the robbers. Or *were* you one of the robbers, too, dressed in those men's trousers and shirt?"

"I refuse to discuss any of this with you," she said stubbornly.

"Do you know where the money is?"

Lupita glared at him.

"Who was the Mexican who got away?" Bolt pressed.

"Does it matter?"

"Maybe. Who was it?"

"His name is Pedro. Pedro Nieves."

"And does Pedro know where the money is hidden?"

"Please, Mr. Bolt, I find you quite rude."

"Or are you the only one who knows where the fifty thousand is hidden?" he continued, pressuring her.

"I've said all I'm going to, Mr. Bolt," she said firmly. "Now, if you'll excuse me." Lupita hiked her skirt up a little so the hem wouldn't drag on the ground and headed for the steps.

"Harmony, go with her," Bolt said. "See if you can help her."

Harmony nodded and caught up with the girl, walked up the steps just behind her. The four harlots, dressed in their tight-fitting, low-cut working gowns, steps aside to let them pass, then followed them into the bordello.

Bolt called Tom and his two ranch hands over.

"Rusty, you and Chet go hitch up the buckboard and bring it out here. I want you to load these bodies on the wagon and then take them into the sheriff in San Antonio. Give him an account of what happened here."

"What about Lupita?" Tom said. "Are you going

to have Chet and Rusty deliver her to the sheriff, too?"

"No. I don't want you to even mention her to the sheriff," he told the cowhands.

Chet and Rusty nodded, then headed for the barn.

"Why not?" Tom argued. "She's a damned thief. She ought to be turned over to the authorities. She ought to be strung up by the neck."

"There's more here than meets the eye," Bolt said cryptically. "And I want her to stick around until I figure it out."

"But, she's a thief, dammit," Tom protested. "I don't like having her around here."

"So what's she going to do? Steal our herd of cattle all by herself?" Bolt laughed.

"I give up on you, Bolt. Every damn time you get involved with a pretty woman, she gets you in a heap of trouble before it's over."

"I ain't involved with Lupita, Tom."

"Not yet, maybe, but you will be, my friend. Just give it time." Tom stalked off to help Chet and Rusty load the dead bodies on the bed of the wagon.

Something caught Bolt's eye just before he turned to go to the bordello. A flicker of white out in the darkness of the yard, someplace near the stable. Something reflecting in the pale moonlight. Something was out there. A man, perhaps.

Suddenly there was the sound of pounding hoofbeats, close by riding away from the ranch. And then Bolt knew. What he'd seen was the flash of white undershorts. He was sure of it. The sound he heard now was that of one of the roans. It was the outlaw riding away. The one who'd escaped earlier.

Instinctively, he went for his gun. He hesitated only long enough to track the sound, which wasn't yet very

46

far away.

He fired into the dark.

The loud roar of his gun deafened him. A puff of white smoke shut off his view.

An instant later he heard the brief scream over the fading, reverberating boom of the gunshot. And a minute later, the low, distant groan.

He smiled and knew he'd gotten off a lucky shot. Damned lucky.

He cocked his head, listened for the thud of a body slamming into the ground.

It didn't come.

All he heard now was the distant sound of the hoofbeats. Faster and faster, softer and softer, until they finally faded away.

"Damn! The bastard got away." he muttered.

"Mighty good shootin', my friend," Tom called out from twenty yards away.

"Not good enough."

Bolt turned, walked up the steps and entered the bordello. Lupita sat on the large, plush sofa across the room. All of the other girls were gathered around her, talking quietly to her. It was a good sign, Bolt thought. Maybe Lupita had confided in the girls.

Cathy Boring, the redheaded harlot, sat on one side of the mestiza, and Doreen Jenson, a tall, natural-looking beauty, sat on the other side. Linda Ramsey stood behind the couch and leaned over, her full breasts nearly spilling out of her low-cut red gown. Winny Hart, the only dark-haired harlot, sat forward on the chair she had pulled over near the couch.

Harmony Sanchez glanced over at Bolt when he came in, then hurried over to meet him.

"Lupita wants to leave right away." Harmony told him privately as the two walked toward the couch.

47

"We're trying to persuade her to stay."

"Are you all right?" Bolt asked Lupita when he stood in front of her.

Lupita stood up. "I'm fine, Mr. Bolt. I've decided to leave tonight."

Bolt saw the flash of wild determination in Lupita's dark eyes and figured that she was more disturbed about her father's death than she wanted to let on.

"Why in the hell would you do a foolish thing like that?" Bolt asked.

"Because I have to," she replied calmly.

"No, you don't. You can wait until morning."

"No, I can't. I'm leaving tonight," she said stubbornly. "Just as soon as I pack my satchel."

"What's your damned hurry?" Bolt snapped.

"I have to finish what my father started. I promised him."

"You mean now that everyone else is dead, you have to recover the robbery money for yourself." Bolt knew it was a rude, unfair remark, but at this point, he didn't care. Lupita was being totally unreasonable. And maybe his words carried more truth than he realized.

"My purpose is none of your concern, Mr. Bolt. Again, thank you for your hospitality." Lupita started to walk away.

"But it's dark out there," Bolt argued. "You might get lost. And there are all sorts of wild animals who roam the prairie at night."

Lupita whirled around to face him.

"I'm not afraid of anything."

"But you can't go tonight. It's too dangerous, I won't let you go."

"You can't stop me, Mr. Bolt. You have no right to hold me here against my will."

48

Bolt shook his head and sighed. He stared down at the braided rug for a minute.

"Listen to me, Lupita," he said as he placed his hands on her arms. "It really would be dangerous for you to ride out there alone tonight, and I'm concerned about you. Whatever your purpose, I'm sure it can wait until morning. Please stay here tonight where you'll be safe."

She looked up at him and the expression in her eyes softened. She hesitated before she spoke.

"All right, Bolt, I'll stay the night."

She changed her mind too quickly, Bolt thought. Maybe she did need his comforting touch after all. Maybe she had an ulterior motive for going along with him, or perhaps, because of the sudden death of her father, she was simply not able to think straight. Whatever the reason, he was glad that she would stay the night.

"Good. I think you need the rest," he said as he withdrew his hands from her arms. He turned and started to walk away.

"Bolt, could I sleep in the big house up on the hill, where you sleep?" she asked.

Her request took him by surprise.

"No, I don't think it would be a good idea, Lupita," he said gently.

"Why? Are you afraid of me? Or are you afraid of yourself, Bolt?" she said sarcastically.

"You flatter yourself, Miss O'Rourke," Bolt said, returning the sarcasm.

"Please, Bolt," she begged. "I'm really scared."

Bolt looked into her eyes and didn't think she was sincere.

"What is it with you, Lupita? One minute you're not afraid of anything and you're ready to go wandering around in the dark by yourself, and suddenly you're too scared to sleep here in this house where you'll be surrounded by people. Where you'll be safe."

"I'm just scared, that's all."

"I'll tell you what I'll do. I'll spend the night out here in the bordello tonight. If Harmony will sleep in one of the upstairs bedrooms, I'll sleep down here in her bed. Would that help?"

Lupita scowled and then her face brightened as she stood up tall and squared her shoulders.

"Oh, I wouldn't want to put you out, Bolt. You go ahead and sleep up in your own house, in your own bed. I'll be just fine here."

Another sudden change of mind on Lupita's part, he thought. He didn't understand the mestiza. Was she deliberately trying to confuse him?

"I really don't mind sleeping down here," he smiled, studying her face for a reaction. "Besides, Harmony's bed is more comfortable than mine."

"Oh? You've slept in her bed before?" Lupita snapped cattily.

Bolt thought he detected a note of jealousy in her voice, but he couldn't be sure. He snagged his gold watch out of his pocket, checked the time. "It's getting late, ladies. I think you'd all better get some sleep. I'll go tell Tom that I'm sleeping in here tonight and I'll be right back." He turned and headed toward the door.

"Bolt?" Lupita called. "I was just wondering. Do you expect me to be a whore?"

He turned his head and looked at her.

"Whatever suits you," he smiled. He walked away, but not before he saw the flash of anger in her eyes.

Bolt heard the slow, rolling creak of the buckboard when he stepped outside. The acrid smell of gunpowder still hung heavy in the air. He scooted down the steps and walked over to Tom just as the wagon was pulling away. He waved at Chet and Rusty, then glanced at the back of the buckboard. A knot of nausea formed in the pit of his stomach when he saw the lumpy blanket on the flat bed and knew that it covered the grizzly mass of bodies. Thick ropes were stretched across the blanket tarp and tied in place to keep the bodies from bouncing off the wagon during the two-mile trip to the sheriff's office in San Antonio.

Tom stood in the middle of the yard, a shovel in his hands. Nearby, two flickering lanterns sat on the ground, and with the light from the lamps and the silvery light from the rising moon, Bolt could see the dark stains where the blood had been spilled. Tom dragged the shovel across the loose dirt several times, covering up one of the larger damp stains.

"You could give me a hand with this," Tom suggested.

"You're doing just fine," Bolt said. "Besides, the exercise will do you good."

"Thanks for nothing," Tom grumbled. "By the way, Joe and Teddy were by a little while ago to get serviced. Hornier than hell, but I guess seein' all them dead bodies scattered on the ground took all the starch out of their peckers. They said they'd come back when it was less hectic around here."

"Good. Hopefully we won't get any more customers tonight. I've already sent the girls to bed."

"Well, if any other horny bastards show up, I'll send them away." Tom glanced around at all the bloodstains he still had to cover. "Looks like I'll be out here most of the night."

"I'm going to sleep down here in the bordello tonight, in Harmony's room. She'll sleep upstairs."

51

"How come?" Tom asked as he moved to another spot and began dragging loose dirt over the dark stain.

"Lupita's scared."

"Don't kid yourself, Bolt. If my hunches are right, that gal ain't afraid of anything. Underneath that soft, warm flesh lies the heart of a goddamned thief. And now she's got all that money to herself. Hell, she probably planned it this way."

"You're being a little hard on her, Tom. We don't know anything about her. Maybe she's just an innocent bystander who got caught up in the rotten world of her father."

"Oh, sure, and the world's flat and people are falling off all the time. I swear, Bolt, when it comes to pretty women, you're totally blind. You let your pecker do your thinking."

"You should talk, Tom."

"I still say you should have turned her over to the authorities."

"Not yet, Tom. I want to keep my eye on her. That's why I'm sleeping down here in the bordello."

"You don't fool me, Bolt. You just want to sneak Lupita out to one of the cottages and put the boots to her."

"Not Lupita, Tom. I don't trust her."

"But I thought you were smitten with her."

"Don't get me wrong, Tom. The way she looks at me with those beautiful dark eyes, I could fall for her in a minute. But there's something about her that bothers me."

"Like what?"

"Like the way her moods change back and forth so quickly. I feel that there's a lot more involved here than just the robbery or the money. Dammit, Lupita just doesn't seem to be the type who would want stolen money, especially in the light of all the deaths it's caused."

"Fifty thousand bucks ain't hay."

"I know. That's what has me confused." Bolt sighed and shook his head again, more puzzled than ever. He turned and walked toward the steps.

"It ain't fair, Bolt," Tom called out.

"It won't take you long to clean up that mess," Bolt said over his shoulder as he climbed the steps. "It'll keep you out of trouble."

"I wasn't talking about that."

Bolt turned to face his friend. "Then what're you griping about now?"

"It just ain't fair, Bolt. While you're in there surrounded by all those beautiful gals, I've gotta sleep up in that big old house all by myself."

"Ahh, you break my heart, Tom. Just remember this," he grinned. "Some of us have what it takes to attract the women, and others, who shall remain nameless, don't. Have sweet dreams, Tom."

The house was quiet when Bolt walked back inside the bordello. The one low-burning coal-oil lamp cast an eerie glow across the long, hushed living room.

He was relieved that the girls had gone to bed and greatful for the quietness in the house. He needed some time to himself now, some thinking time. He felt his shoulders sag as he allowed himself to relax for the first time since early morning when he'd met with the damned cattle buyers.

He walked over and blew into the lantern, extinguished the low flame, then made his way through the darkness to Harmony's bedroom at the back of the house.

The bedroom was dimly lit by the flickering orange

glow from the lantern on the dresser, the wick of the lantern carefully turned down just so by Harmony's loving hands, he knew. He was pleased to see that she had also turned down the covers of her big featherbed for him, and placed a glass of drinking water on the nightstand. Harmony was thoughtful that way, always sensitive to his needs, always trying to please him without putting any pressure on him to return the favor.

He felt comfortable in Harmony's room, with all its feminine touches, its row of perfume bottles on the dressing table, its hand-painted pitcher and bowl, the curtained closet where her fancy gowns hung, the pink curtains at the window, and the pink satin comforter on the bed. He knew that her filmy night-gowns and undergarments were tucked neatly away in a dresser drawer, and that her hairbrush and makeup were stored out of sight on a shelf behind the curtain of her dressing table.

Yes, he'd slept in this room with Harmony before, but only in the daytime when there was nobody else in the house. When the other girls were gone to town for the day, or when they were out riding the horses.

He placed his Stetson on the dresser, leaned over to blow out the lantern. As he walked across the room he drank in the delicate fragrance of her perfumes. He removed his gunbelt and holster, hung it over the bedpost. He sat on the edge of the bed, tugged his boots off, then stripped out of his trousers and chambray shirt. Finally, wearing only his shorts and socks, and totally exhausted from the day's events, he climbed into bed and felt the softness of the bed engulf him as he sank down into it.

But sleep didn't come right away. He stared up at the ceiling for a long, long time, trying to figure

Lupita out, trying to keep his feelings for the girl separate from his logical, common-sense thinking. It wasn't easy.

Finally, with the covers in shambles from his tossing and turning, Bolt drifted into a shallow sleep.

Sometime later, he was awakened abruptly by a noise. It took him a minute to get his bearings and remember where he was, but it took him only a brief instant to realize that he was not alone in the room.

Chapter Five

Bolt tensed, his eyes wide open. He held his breath, dared not to move a muscle.

Pale beams of moonlight filtered through the sheer pink curtains at the window and bathed the darkened bedroom with a hazy silver glow.

He blinked his eyes and strained to see across the room. When he saw the vague shadow near the door of the far wall, where the room was the darkest, his heard skipped a beat. His hands turned sweaty when he heard the soft click as the door closed tight. Without moving any other part of his body, he started to ease his hand back up over his shoulder to the bedpost, where his pistol hung in its holster. He wished now that he'd removed the weapon from the holster and stuffed it under his pillow where he could reach it without too much effort or movement.

The figure stepped away from the door, started across the room. Bolt saw the feminine shape of the nightgown, the flowing lines of the light robe, the puff of blond hair that looked gray in the dim light of the moon.

"Harmony?" he whispered.

"Quiet, Bolt," Harmony whispered.

Bolt heard the rustle of her gown as she tiptoed

across the room, smelled the heady aroma of her delicate scent as she came closer. She didn't speak again until she stood next to the bed.

"I had to wait until the other girls were asleep."

Bolt propped himself up on his elbow.

"What time is it?"

"After midnight," she said, keeping her voice low. "I thought that girl, Lupita, would never get to sleep. She must have paced the floor for thirty minutes before she finally went to bed, and then I heard her tossing and turning for a long time after that."

"I'm sure she's upset about her father."

"Well, everything's quiet up there now, thank God. There's just you and me."

"Is there something wrong?"

"Nothing that you can't take care of," she whispered in a low, sultry voice.

She slipped the light robe from her shoulders, let it fall to the floor where it nestled in a soft heap on the braided rug. Her hard nipples jutted against the thin fabric of her nightgown, stretched it taut. Bolt peered through the filmy material and saw the dark thatch between her legs, which was just inches away from his face. A warm rush flooded his loins.

"You wanton hussy," he teased.

"Yes, I am. I've been lying up there thinking about you for more than an hour, until I couldn't stand it any longer. Just knowing you were down here in my bed."

She pulled her nightgown up over her head and dropped it on top of her robe. Bolt reached over and placed his hand between her legs, feeling her warmth. That was one of the things he liked about being with Harmony. He could be natural with her. He could touch her there and know that she would respond like

57

a woman, that she wouldn't play the coy games that some women played. They both knew what they wanted and there was no need for her to play the shy, innocent little girl.

"And you're very bold to come here, with so many people in the house," he said, and there was a raspy husk to his voice.

"Not so bold. Just hot for your body. But never fear, everyone else is asleep. Before I tiptoed down here, I stood in the hallway and listened for several minutes, just to make sure. And you'd better fix that step that squeaks. I almost forgot and stepped on it."

"You sneaky wench," he laughed.

"You'd better be grateful, Bolt. After all, I wouldn't want to set a bad example for the other girls. They might get jealous and attack you en masse."

"A bachelor's dream come true," Bolt grinned.

"Don't you wish?"

"No, you're enough woman for me, Harmony."

"Too much, likely."

"Never." He took his hand away, threw the sheet back and quickly slipped out of his undershorts, tossed them aside. He leaned back on the bed. Harmony crawled in bed with him, scooted over until their bodies came together in an explosion of heat. The touch of her burning hand sent a shock of electricity through his body and he felt the goose-bumps rise on his naked flesh.

"Oh, Harmony," he croaked, "you know how to do it to me."

"I haven't done anything yet," she whispered in his ear. "Just wait."

The feel of her hot, tickling breath against his ear sent another wave of goosebumps across his flesh.

"I'm waiting."

And then she was on him like a wild tiger, ravaging his mouth with hot kisses, peppering his face with her wet, sensual lips. Harmony was the best there was. She knew when to ease up, when to pause in order to stay his climax, when to start her tender manipulations again. She sensed his every need, his every whim, as if they were two people linked together with but one mind, one heart. He had made love to Harmony more times than he could count and yet he never tired of her. She was always fresh, always new in her approach.

"Oh, you do it to me," he said, his voice cracking with a husk as brittle as dried flowers.

"I hope so." She slid a leg over one of his.

Bolt thought he heard a noise in the house. A brief, faint sound, a distant creaking noise, as if the house were settling on its foundation. Not an uncommon sound, but still, it was enough to alert his senses. He tensed, held his breath. Maybe it had been the chiming of the grandfather clock in the living room, or perhaps a mouse had scurried across the kitchen.

"Stop," he whispered. "Listen."

"What's the matter?"

"Shhh. I thought I heard something."

The couple remained completely motionless for a full minute. Bolt cocked his head and listened carefully, but didn't hear anything more.

"I guess it was nothing," he said.

"What was it?" Harmony whispered near his ear. "What did you hear?"

"I guess it was probably the living room clock striking one o'clock. Could it be that late already?"

"Yes, it's about that time."

Bolt placed his hand on her cheeks, drew her head down close to his, and they both forgot about the brief

59

interruption. He brushed his lips against hers several times, teasing her with near-kisses, then kissed her full on the mouth.

Her full, warm breasts crushed against his chest as she slid her probing tongue into his mouth. She found his tongue and flicked her own across it, tantalizing him with her playful movements. He slid his hand down and cupped a breast in his palm, massaged it. He felt her response in her wet, passionate kiss.

"I want you," he said breathlessly when they broke the kiss.

"Not yet," she whispered.

She shifted positions, bent her head to take him in. The wet heat of her consuming mouth drove Bolt into a state of mindless frenzy.

"Yes, oh yes," he cried.

Long minutes later, he rolled off of her, totally spent. They lay together for a long time basking in the afterglow of their lovemaking, neither wanting to talk, neither feeling the need to talk. The musk of their twin passions filled the room, mingled with the scents of her perfume. The moonlight glistened off his limp mass of flesh as the air cooled them and began to dry their sweaty bodies.

"I'd better get back upstairs," Harmony said, finally, as she scooted to the edge of the bed and sat up.

"I wish you wouldn't," he said, grabbing for her hand.

"I really wish I didn't have to go," she whispered, "but it would never do if the girls woke up in the morning and found me here." She withdrew her hand from his, stood up, and pulled her thin nightgown over her head, tugging it down into place.

"They know we sleep together," Bolt said.

"Yes, up in the ranch house. But not down here,

not with them here in the house, anyway."

"You're right, I know," he sighed, "but it doesn't make it any easier for me to let you go. I needed you tonight, Harmony."

She slipped her hand into the sleeve of her light robe, pulled it up over her shoulder, then slid her other arm into the sleeve. "I know. Sneaky, weren't we?" she smiled. "Maybe that's why it was so special tonight. The forbidden fruit."

"It's special every time we're together."

She buttoned her robe, leaned over, and gave him a quick kiss. She tiptoed across the room and silently closed the bedroom door after she left. He leaned back into the pillow and listened for her retreating footsteps. He heard only the faintest scuffles of her bare feet just outside his room and then he heard nothing more.

He smiled as he pictured her sneaking up the stairs, trying to keep from stepping on the plank that squeaked. He'd have to remember to fix that board in the morning if he planned to spend another night in the bordello.

Harmony was just as cautious about sneaking back upstairs as she'd been sneaking down, although it really didn't matter now. If one of the girls saw her wandering around the house, she could explain that she'd heard a noise and had come to investigate. Not that they'd believe her. The harlots knew her too well.

She carefully avoided the step that creaked, the third one from the top, and promised herself that she'd remind Bolt to fix it in the morning.

With eight small bedrooms leading off of the long, narrow hall, four on each side, the upstairs hallway was pitch black. When Harmony reached the top step, she was startled to see a small slice of silver moonlight reflecting off the polished hardwood floor. The dim gray light came from the last bedroom down the hall, and she saw that the bedroom door was open a few inches.

She caught her breath and stood perfectly still. That was the room where Lupita slept. Had the mestiza snuck away into the night while Harmony was downstairs with Bolt? Harmony listened closely and could barely hear the slight shuffling of feet within the room. There were sounds, too, but all too faint for her to make out. The rustle of clothing? The flutter of paper? The muffled clank of an object on the dresser? The dribble of water being poured slowly from the pitcher into the bowl or into a glass? The whisper of something being moved around? Harmony couldn't tell.

Maybe Lupita was not feeling well and was searching through her things for some tonic. Had the girl heard her go downstairs earlier? Had Lupita herself snuck down and listened at Harmony's bedroom door while Bolt and Harmony were locked in a lovers' embrace? Why was the girl's door slightly ajar? Harmony had no way of telling.

She took short, slow steps down the hall, meticulously placing one foot in front of the other, praying that none of the hardwood boards would creak under her weight.

She inched her way along the hall, picking up one bare foot at a time, putting it down slowly slightly ahead of the other, testing the floor plank before she shifted her weight. She got closer and closer to the open door.

The clock downstairs chimed once and she nearly

jumped out of her skin. She clamped her hands to her pounding chest, caught her breath, then wondered if Lupita had heard her slapping her chest, a thumping sound that now seemed to magnify in Harmony's ears.

She had no idea what the girl was up to this time of the night, but she knew that Lupita had been wearing a pistol when she'd first arrived that afternoon and that she was determined to have her own way.

Harmony waited a minute and then, satisfied that she'd not been heard, she continued to sneak down the hall to Lupita's open door. She tucked herself against the wall where the moonlight wouldn't hit her and tipped her head out just far enough to peer into the room.

She was startled when she saw the girl. Lupita dressed in the same grimy trousers and the same tattered man's shirt that she had been wearing when Harmony had first seen her. Lupita's long, dark hair took on a ghostly sheen from the sparse moonlight that penetrated the bedroom curtain.

Because of her position as she hugged the wall outside of the bedroom, Harmony's line of vision was limited. She could see only a small, triangular-shaped portion of the room, the closest corner which consisted of about a fourth of the room. From her angle, she saw the small table near the door, where an unlit lantern always stood. She had a full view of the dresser against the wall, but could only see part of the dressing table, a corner of the cushioned stool in front of it, and the edge of the mirror that hung above the table.

Harmony noticed that the girl's pistol and holster were lying on the chest of drawers near the porcelain pitcher and bowl. There were other items on the dresser, but Harmony couldn't tell what they were. She also saw the shape of Lupita's dark felt hat where it sat on the small dressing table.

At first glance, it seemed to Harmony that Lupita was restlessly pacing the floor again, walking from the dresser to where the bed would be, then marching back to the chest of drawers or the low dressing table. Because the room was only dimly lit by the light of the moon, it took Harmony a minute to realize that each time Lupita turned from the dresser to pace toward the bed, she was carrying something in her hands. When the girl marched back toward the chest of drawers, her hands were by her sides, empty.

Harmony watched two full cycles of the girl's pacing, and then, the next time Lupita whirled around and headed toward the bed, Harmony stuck her head out a little farther so she could see more of the room. She saw Lupita's open carpetbag on the bed. The bed itself was made up, covers smooth, as if the mestiza had never slept in it.

Lupita wasn't pacing the floor, Harmony suddenly realized. The girl was packing her satchel. Lupita was planning to sneak away in the middle of the night, just like the thief Harmony figured she was.

Harmony watched the girl only long enough to see her pick up her hat from the dressing table, set it back down, and lean into the mirror as she gathered up her long hair and pushed it to the top of her head.

Lupita turned her head suddenly as she glanced over at the pistol on the chest of drawers. Harmony held her breath, drew her head back, tucked in her chin, and hoped that Lupita hadn't seen her.

Harmony didn't wait long. When she heard Lupita make another trip to the bed, she snuck away from the room. As she padded silently along the hallway, she wondered if Lupita had the stolen money in her carpetbag.

In her haste to tell Bolt of her discovery, Harmony almost stepped on the squeaky step as she made her way down the stairs. She caught herself just in time, then almost tripped as she extended her foot out to the next step.

By the time Harmony reached the downstairs bedroom, her heart was beating faster than a hummingbird's wings.

Chapter Six

Basking in the glow of contentment, Bolt had fallen asleep shortly after Harmony had left the room. He hadn't bothered to put his undershorts on.

This time he didn't hear her enter the bedroom. He didn't wake up until she was standing over him, whispering his name.

"Bolt. Bolt, wake up."

He stirred, opened his eyes.

"Harmony? What is it?" he mumbled, then closed his eyes and started to drift off to sleep again.

"Bolt, are you awake?" Harmony gently shook his shoulder.

"Yeah," he said as he blinked his eyes. He grinned up at her when he saw that she was still wearing her sheer nightgown. "Am I dreaming, woman, or did you come back for seconds?"

"Bolt, please. It's Lupita. She's leaving."

Bolt's head popped up like a shot and he quickly rolled to the edge of the bed. His arm dangled over the side as he snatched his undershorts from the floor. He slipped them on, then sat up on the edge of the bed.

"Is it morning already?" he asked as he tried to

shake the cobwebs of sleep from his mind.

"No. It's still the middle of the night. It's just a little after one o'clock. She's up there now, packing her bag and getting ready to leave. You've got to stop her, Bolt."

"Why bother?" Bolt grumbled. "If the thievin' little bitch wants to leave, let her go. Maybe the wolves will eat her up."

"You don't mean that, Bolt, and you know it."

"I know, but right now, it seems like a good idea," he grumbled. "Hell, I don't owe that half-breed little hussy anything."

"You like her, don't you, Bolt?" Harmony asked, with no malice intended.

"I'm confused about her. She just doesn't seem like the kind of a girl who would be involved in a bank robbery, and yet, I know she is. And how can anyone who looks so sweet and innocent be so damned bull-headed? Greed, is all I can figure."

"Where do you think the money's hidden?" Harmony asked as she handed Bolt his shirt.

"I don't know." He stood up, slipped his arms in the shirt, buttoned the front. "Hell, it could be anyplace from here to Austin."

"Do you think there's a chance that she's got it in her carpetbag? Just a thought."

Bolt thought a minute. "No, I don't think so. That much cash would weigh quite a bit, and her satchel didn't seem to be that heavy."

"Bolt, please hurry up," Harmony said as she scooped his trousers off the floor and handed them to him. "Lupita was putting her hat on when I left. She's almost ready to leave."

"If she'd confess what she knows about the rob-

67

bery, we might be able to help her, but if she leaves here, the law'll track her down."

"It's their job, Bolt, not yours. You should've turned her over to the authorities in the first place instead of insisting that she stay here."

"You sound just like Tom," Bolt grumbled. He stepped into his trousers, tugged them up in place.

"Hurry, Bolt," Harmony whispered. "She could come downstairs any minutes."

"I'm hurrying," he muttered. He tugged on his boots. He snatched the gunbelt from the bedpost, wrapped it around his waist, fastened the buckle, adjusted the holster, started for the door.

Harmony grabbed his arm.

"Bolt, be careful," she cried.

"I will."

"She might be desperate, Bolt, and she's got a gun."

"I know."

"Bolt, if she's got the money with her and you try to stop her, she might try to shoot it out. Please be careful," she pleaded.

They both heard the noise. The creaking of the step, third from the top. The bedroom door was open now and the sound more distinct.

"Hurry, Bolt, hurry!" Harmony cried. "She's going to get away."

"Damn," Bolt muttered. He thought about it for only an instant and figured that Lupita would go out the front door and head for the stable to get a horse. He knew that if she were sneaking through the dark house, which was unfamiliar to her, it could take her two or three minutes to reach the front door.

Maybe, just maybe, if he hurried, he could be there

waiting for her when she stepped out onto the porch.

He dashed out of the bedroom, took a few steps to the kitchen door, which was open. He made little noise as he took quick, long strides across the kitchen floor to the back door. He eased the bolt out of its cradle, opened the door, and didn't take the time to close it after he'd stepped outside in the darkness.

He snuck around the bordello, avoiding the bushes and trees that he knew were in the path. He made his way around to the front corner of the house, where he stopped and glanced up at the porch, glad that he'd left the porch lantern burning. Lupita wasn't on the porch, but he was confident that he'd beaten her there.

He debated whether to dash up on the porch and be waiting for her when she came though the door, quickly deciding against the idea. If he stayed in the shadows of the house, he could use the light from the lantern to his advantage if she decided to draw her gun against him. He had no way of knowing how good a shot she was, but she was tough, and perhaps, because she'd ridden with the outlaws, she was better with a pistol than most men. In the darkness, he would be an invisible target.

He hoped it wouldn't come to a gun battle with Lupita. He didn't want to hurt her. Yes, Harmony was right about his liking the mestiza. Right now, he just wanted to help her, before it was too late for her, before she was tracked down and shot by an anxious lawman or a greedy bounty hunter. If it came to a duel between the two of them, he knew he could kill her and be justified, because she was an outlaw. But he didn't want to. He would just wait until she started across the yard to the stable and then run out and grab her before she knew he was there.

He tensed when he heard the clatter of the door-knob being turned slowly. He moved slightly to his right and tucked in behind a bush that was as tall as he was so that there was no chance of her spotting him.

He waited as the door creaked open, inch by inch. He saw Lupita step out on the porch, carpetbag in hand, then turn to close the door behind her.

Even though Harmony had told him that Lupita was wearing the old, rumpled men's clothing, he was shocked by the sight of her. She was no longer the beautiful, dark-haired girl with the twinkling eyes whom he'd talked to on the porch last evening. Gone was the pretty blue dress that looked royally purple in the lamp glow. Gone were the enticing curves of her body, the rounded mounds of her breasts pressing against her fabric. Dressed in the grubby clothes and battered felt hat, and with the pistol slung low on her hip, she looked every bit the part of a hardened outlaw.

There were two sides to Lupita, and Bolt didn't like the one he was seeing now.

The wooden planks creaked as the mestiza snuck across the porch, and Bolt saw her cringe with each squeak.

Bolt's breath caught in his throat when he heard a noise out in the yard. The crunch of a twig, he thought. He whirled his head around and stared out into the yard. He saw only the shadowy trees that were always there. As he peered at each tree, searching for something else, he swore the trees moved. He let his breath out slowly, knowing the night was playing tricks on his mind.

He glanced up at Lupita and knew that she had heard the sound, too. She stood perfectly still at the top of the steps and scanned the dark yard.

Bolt heard another noise and turned his head just in time to see a man step out of the darkness and into the circle of light that spilled onto the ground from the porch lantern.

"Lupita," the man said and Bolt detected the Spanish accent.

Bolt wondered who the stranger was. Someone who knew Lupita, obviously. Not one of the bandits. They were all dead. Or were they, he wondered. Hadn't Sheriff Cotter said that he'd expected to find eight horses?

A stunned expression came over Lupita's dark face.

"Jose? Jose Contreras?" she said in a loud whisper.

"Yes, it is Jose. Does it surprise you to see me, little one?"

"Yes, yes it does," Lupita stammered. "What are you doing here?"

"I came here to see you, my little friend." The Mexican laughed viciously.

"I'm not your friend, Jose."

"Ah, but you could be, *mi señorita bonita*," he sneered. "With all that money you have, you and I, we make a good team. Yes?"

"No. I don't have the money." Lupita turned around and glanced nervously at the house, as if she were afraid of awakening somebody inside. "Go away, Jose."

"Not until I get the money."

"You already have your share. Papa already paid you," she protested.

"Not enough, my little pretty. Your father, he does

71

not count so well."

When Bolt saw the Mexican take a couple of steps closer to the porch, he slid his hand over to his holster and rested it on the butt of his pistol.

"That's not true," Lupita said in a hushed voice. "My father paid you every penny he promised you."

"It is not enough, Lupita. I have need for more. I will take half of what is left and you may have the rest. That is fair, yes?"

"I told you, I don't have the money."

"But you know where it is hidden, my pretty lady," the outlaw snarled. "Now that your father is dead, you are the only one who knows where the money is. And you are going to tell me. Yes?"

"How did you know Papa is dead?" she said, a sudden hardness to her voice.

"I drink the mescal at the cantina in San Antonio when they bring the bodies in. I see them," he laughed. "All of them. All except Pedro Nieves. Where is Pedro, Lupita? Do you go to meet him now?"

It was a thought that Bolt hadn't thought of.

"No, Jose. I thought Pedro was dead with the others. How did you know where to find me out here?"

"Ah, that is the easy part, my pretty lady."

Bolt saw the Mexican twirl the ends of his moustache and he wanted to blow the sonofabitch away.

"When they bring that many bodies to town," Contreras said, "word spreads fast. I listen to the talk. I leave right away to find you and the money."

"You will not get more money from me," Lupita said, with the same determination Bolt had heard before.

"I think you will change your mind when you hear what I have to tell you," Jose said as he swaggered closer to the steps. "Fidel and Juan, they still drink the mescal at the cantina. *Muy borracho.* When they learn that I am gone, they will come here to look for you. They will want the money, too, you know. You and I, we do not give them any. We keep it for ourselves. yes?"

Who were Fidel and Juan, Bolt wondered. More outlaws who had helped pull off the Austin bank robbery? It sounded like it from what the filthy Mexican was saying. If so, there were still at least four bandits alive that Lupita O'Rourke would have to contend with. He wondered if she realized what her odds were if she had to run from the bandits, as well as the lawmen who were sure to come looking for her, and the bounty hunters who would track her for a share of the money. Not very good, he imagined. Not unless she was a hell of a lot stronger than he thought she was.

"You're a snake, Jose," Lupita spit.

"Not a snake, Lupita. A fox. You and I will be very happy together. Yes?"

"No."

"Where is the money, Lupita? Do you carry it there in your little bag?"

"In this?" Lupita held the carpetbag out in front of her. "No, Jose, I have no money in this little bag," she laughed. "I carry nothing but my personal things in this satchel."

"Throw the bag down and let me see for myself." Contreras demanded. "I have no trust for you."

"No." Lupita leaned over and plunked the satchel down on the porch beside her. When she brought her

73

hand back up, she let it rest on the butt of her pistol. "If you want this old satchel, Jose, you come and get it."

Jose Contreras didn't take her challenge.

"Where is the money, Lupita?"

Bolt watched as Contreras slowly drew his pistol out of his holster and brushed his hand slowly across the shiny barrel, as if wiping dust from it. Bolt was prepared to shoot the bastard.

"It's buried. Deep in the ground. You'll never find it, Jose," Lupita said stubbornly. "None of you will ever find it."

"I will be forced to kill you, Lupita, if you do not tell me where the money is."

Bolt heard the change in the Mexican's voice, the anger that boiled beneath the surface. He eased his pistol halfway out of its holster, held it there. He glanced up at the dark house and hoped that none of the girls lit a lantern in there or came to the window to stare out at the commotion just then. Contreras was a keg of gunpowder and any small spark could set him off.

"You are very stupid, Jose." Lupita brought her hand up away from the pistol and folded her arms across her chest. She tossed her head back and laughed at the threatening Mexican. "It would do you little good to kill me. If I were dead, then you and your filthy friends would not know where to look for the money."

Bolt winced at her words, her mocking laughter. Damn, that girl had guts. Or she had no feelings at all. It was hard to tell. He wished she'd just tell the Mexican where the money was and let it go at that. Before there was more bloodshed. How could she risk

74

her life like this? The money couldn't mean that much to her.

"Go on, kill me," Lupita taunted. "Then you and your stinking friends will spend the rest of your miserable lives like the dogs you are, on your hands and knees, digging for bones and finding nothing."

"You tempt me, bitch," Contreras shouted.

"Do it, Jose," Lupita pushed. "Kill me and you will die on your hands and knees before you find the money."

Bolt saw the Mexican's body stiffen and sensed his fury. He knew that Contreras was using every bit of strength he had to control his violent temper. In the Mexican's value system, Bolt knew, it would not be considered manly if he gave in to the woman's demands, no matter what they were.

"If you are dead, it will not matter at all to us, Lupita," Contreras said casually, his calm, even voice hiding the anger that raged inside. "We already know that your father did not hide the money until after he gave us our pay in San Antonio. It was at noon yesterday. You remember. Yes?"

"Yes, I remember. Papa paid each of you five hundred dollars for your work. That was your price."

"It was not enough. I figure there are over forty-six thousand greenbacks left. If you do not wish to share it with me, then I will take it for myself."

"Shoot me, then, and you can have it all." Lupita eased her hand back to her pistol and glared at him. "All you have to do is find it."

"San Antonio is not such a big town that we cannot find the money without your help."

Contreras stroked the gun barrel again, then slowly brought the pistol up and aimed it at Lupita. He didn't have his finger around the trigger. He moved his head slightly, sighted in on her, as if he was practicing the ritual.

Bolt watched him carefully, saw the man thumb the hammer back. Contreras slid his finger around the trigger, using slow, deliberate motions so the girl would see him. Lupita was pushing her luck, Bolt thought. All the bandit had to do now was pull the trigger.

"You're a stupid fool, Jose. You're an ugly Mexican," Lupita called out in her mocking voice, continuing to ridicule the outlaw bandit.

Bolt felt the tension building. He could almost see the rage mounting within the outlaw as Jose struggled to stay in control.

"Look who calls me names," Contreras said, his strong, steady voice beginning to crack. "The filthy, half-breed whore."

Lupita didn't stop her vicious verbal attack.

"You know about whores, don't you, Jose?" she yelled. "They won't let you near them. Even if you have all the money in the world, there is not a woman alive who will sleep with you."

Jose's temper exploded then.

"You filthy little bitch," he shouted.

The bandit's finger quickly curled around the trigger, squeezed.

Bolt thumbed the hammer back as he snaked his pistol out of its holster. He stepped out away from the bush, fired as he brought the weapon up.

Three shots boomed through the night air, fired so close in time that it sounded like a giant explosion. Fired so close together that it was hard to tell whether two or three bullets had been shot.

At the very instant Bolt fired his gun, he saw the Mexican's tall body jerk backward as a bullet crashed into his chest. Bolt knew instantly that his bullet had not been the one to kill Cantreras.

He glanced up and saw Lupita standing on the porch, her body rigid, her gaze straight ahead, her stiff arm still extended out in front of her, smoke still curling up from the pistol in her hand.

Bolt was amazed. It had been an even draw, and Lupita, the beautiful, diminutive, delicate girl, had outshot them all.

Chapter Seven

Now that he'd seen the mestiza shoot, Bolt was
even more hesitant about approaching the girl, trying
to talk some sense into her.

An even draw? It hadn't been that, really. Since
Contreras, the Mexican outlaw, already had his pistol
cocked and aimed, his finger curled around the trigger before the showdown came, and Bolt had had his
weapon halfway out of its holster, it was Lupita who'd
had the disadvantage. And yet, she'd drawn her pistol
and fired before either of the men could get a shot off.

Bolt wondered if the fact that the Mexican had
been drinking mescal had slowed his reactions. But
there was no excuse for Bolt not to have beaten the girl
in the draw. Bolt was fast, a true shot, and it had
taken him only a split-second to step out away from
the bushes and fire. Evidently, it was the split-second
that Lupita needed to outshoot him. And Lupita had
shot as cold-heartedly as any hardened outlaw Bolt
had ever seen.

It didn't matter how. Contreras was dead and that
was what counted. Bolt was just glad that he hadn't
been the one to go up against Lupita's gun. And yet it
could still happen. He could still face her in a
showdown if she wouldn't listen to him.

The girl hadn't moved yet. Her gun had stopped smoking several minutes ago and still she hadn't moved. Her rigid body remained poised in a shooting stance, her arm still extended out in front of her, the hand that held the pistol steady as a rock. Her gaze was fixed somewhere out in the darkness of the yard, beyond the circle of light that fell on the ground from the porch lamp, as if she were waiting for someone else to show up.

Was she peering out into the darkness, searching for Bolt? Searching for someone else to kill? He didn't know. Did she even know he was there? Had she heard the almost simultaneous explosion of three separate shots, or did she think there were only hers and the Mexican outlaw's? Had she seen him in the shadow of the house when he'd stepped out to shoot at the outlaw? He couldn't be sure.

Bolt wondered if he should forget about talking to Lupita and just let her go. She wasn't his responsibility. Let the lawmen track her down, if the remaining bandits didn't find her first.

No, he couldn't let her run away to face such insurmountable odds. She was fast and true with the gun, but sooner or later, someone would take her out. And there was more to her than the cold-hearted woman he saw standing on the porch now, poised pistol in her hand. He'd seen the other side of her, the gentle, caring side, the night before. She was a driven woman, and he didn't understand the reasons behind her fierce determination. He only knew that it had to be more than the money.

As he watched her standing there on the porch, he saw that her eyes didn't move, but remained fixed in one position, glazed over, as if she were too stunned to move, as if she were in a hypnotic trance. If he approached her, she just might turn and fire on him, but he had to try.

He kept his pistol in his hand, stayed in the shadows of the house as he made his way over the edge of the porch. Still, she did not move. He eased over to the bottom of the steps where the light from the porch lamp shone down on him and he was in full view of the girl. She didn't see him. Her eyes remained fixed.

"Lupita," he called gently.

She blinked her eyes once, but showed no signs that she had heard him call to her. With the pistol still clutched in her hand, her extended arm wavered only slightly.

He saw that the trigger wasn't cocked and decided to go for it. He edged up the steps sideways, letting his back slide along the hand railing to keep himself balanced. He kept his pistol low by his side, slightly behind his leg where it was out of sight.

When he reached the top of the steps and was only a few feet away from the dazed girl, he hesitated, watched her carefully for some reaction. When she still didn't move, he scurried around behind her and stuffed his gun into its holster.

"Lupita, it's over," he said gently as he slid his hand along the bottom of her arm and quickly grabbed the hand that clutched the pistol. He held her hand firmly so she couldn't turn on him.

It was when he touched her arm and spoke softly in her ear that he felt Lupita's fragile body relax and sink back against his chest.

"It's over, Lupita," he repeated as he eased the pistol from her limp hand and stuffed it into the top of his trousers.

"Oh, my God, I've killed a man," Lupita cried. She spun around and looked at Bolt, the expression in her eyes filled with a sudden horror.

He took her in his arms and held her tight, felt her

body shudder against his. She buried her head into his chest and began to sob. When her hat toppled off of her head, her dark locks tumbled to her heaving shoulders, taking on a sheen from the light. She seemed so small and delicate in his arms just then, so frail, that Bolt couldn't help but hold her tight as he ran his fingers through her hair and patted her on the head as if she were a child. No matter what else Lupita was, she was a warm, sensitive woman.

The bordello door creaked open behind him. Bolt glanced over his shoulder and saw Harmony peeking out. She nodded her understanding.

Lupita's sobbing finally subsided and Bolt was just about to take her inside when he heard the sound of running footsteps off to his left. He gently pushed Lupita into the house where Harmony took her by the arm. He scooped up her carpetbag, tossed it inside, then closed the door.

Bolt drew his gun, thumbed the hammer back, as he dashed to the edge of the porch where the light wouldn't be directly on him. He peered into the darkness.

"What in the hell's going on down there?" Tom Penrod's voice boomed out of the dark. "You shootin' rabid skunks or something?" he said as he appeared below Bolt.

"You might say that," Bolt said dryly as he slipped his gun back into the holster. "You could get yourself killed that way, Tom, bursting out of the dark like that. My fingers are itchy tonight."

Tom noticed the dead man on the ground. "Yair, I reckon they are itchy. Looks like we got another body to cart to town."

"It can wait till morning."

"What'd you kill him with? A damned cannon?" Tom asked. "That shot was so loud, it rattled my bed."

"There were three shots fired at the same time, Tom, but I didn't kill him."

"He looks dead to me."

"Lupita killed him."

"Lupita?" Tom said, his voice filled with amazement. "She's some little spitfire, ain't she?"

"I reckon."

"Who is he?" Tom nodded toward the body.

"One of the bank robbers who came looking for the money."

Tom walked over and took a closer look at the bloody body. "It ain't that feller who high-tailed it out of here in his shorts, is it?"

"No. It seems there were more bandits than we thought there were," Bolt sighed.

"Shit. How many more?"

"I don't know. Two or three, maybe. I'm going to go in and talk to Lupita now. You want to join me?"

"Hell, no, I'm gonna go back up to the house where it's safe."

"Coward," Bolt grinned.

"Damned right, and if I was you, I'd get rid of that gal as soon as possible. You keep Lupita here and she'll draw the outlaws like mosquitoes."

"You ain't me, Tom. Goodnight."

"Just don't go shootin' off anymore cannons tonight," Tom grumbled as he headed for the house on the hill. "I need my sleep."

"I'll try, Tom."

Bolt turned and went inside. Two lanterns had been lit and all of the girls hovered around Lupita, just as they'd done after her father had died. It didn't surprise him to see that the girls were awake. He walked over closer to the grouping of furniture and saw that Lupita was still badly shaken by the ordeal.

The mestiza sat in the big, overstuffed chair, her worn carpetbag in her lap. She stared aimlessly at the rug, a sad, haunted expression in her eyes. She toyed with the strands of her hair as if she needed something to occupy her hands.

"Oh, Bolt, I was so worried about you," Harmony Sanchez cried as she dashed over to Bolt. She threw her arms around him, hugged him tight.

Bolt noticed Lupita's head jerk up, saw the flash of anger in her dark eyes as she glared up at him. Anger born of jealousy, he thought, as he saw her glance briefly at Harmony and then tighten her lips. Harmoney's affectionate hug was a perfectly normal reaction under the circumstances and nothing for Lupita to get upset about, even if she had taken a fancy to him, which he doubted. He didn't understand the girl's swift change of moods, probably never would. But at least she was showing that she still felt some emotion, and that was a good sign.

"Nothing to worry about," Bolt smiled as Harmony stood back to look at him.

"You don't know what it's like to stand in here and listen to everything and not know what's going to happen. And when the girls came downstairs all upset, I had to keep them quiet. Keep them from lighting a lamp."

"Thanks for that."

"You don't know how my heart sank when I heard that loud blast," Harmony sighed. "I was scared to death to open the door. I thought I'd find you dead."

"You worry too much, Harmony," he smiled. "Why don't you and the other girls go on back to bed. I want to talk to Lupita for a few minutes."

Bolt walked closer to Lupita as the girls filed up the stairs.

"Are you all right?" he asked. He saw the expression in her eyes soften.

"Yes, I think so," she said as she shuddered. "I've never killed anybody before."

"I didn't think so."

"It's a terrible feeling, knowing that he'll never live again."

"I know. It can tear you up inside."

"Jose was bad, Bolt, very bad, but I had no right to take his life away from him."

"He would have killed you if you hadn't. You had no choice."

"But I murdered him." Lupita covered her eyes with her hand. "I can't believe I murdered someone. I could be arrested for murder."

"You had to do it, Lupita. When we deliver the body to the sheriff in the morning, we'll be sure and tell him that you fired in self-defense. I can testify to it. You won't be held responsible for it."

"Oh, no, Bolt," she said. "Whatever you do, don't take Jose's body to town. Bury him here. Please."

"Why?"

"If the others find out he's dead, they'll come after me," she said as she clutched the carpetbag in her lap. "They want that money."

"It's stolen money," Bolt said, a sudden harshness to his voice. "If you know where it is, Lupita, you'd better turn it in."

"I can't. I promised my father on his deathbed." She glared up at Bolt.

"You don't owe him anything. He was a thief."

Lupita sat up tall. She slammed the carpetbag to the floor beside her feet, then sat up on the edge of the chair, looking like she wanted to savagely attack Bolt. Her eyes glittered with sparks of anger.

"You don't know anything about my father," she snapped. "He was a kind and gentle man, a loving

84

father. He was totally devoted to my mother. How dare you say anything about him."

"He was a thief."

"That doesn't make him a bad person," Lupita argued vehemently.

"In my book, it does."

"Well, maybe you're reading the wrong book," she spat. "You can't see beyond the cover. You don't have the ability to look into a person's heart and see their goodness."

Her words stung. Maybe she was right. Maybe he'd gotten so tough-skinned with the things he'd seen over the years that he could no longer tell what a person was really like. Maybe he didn't take the time to find out.

"Maybe your father was the best man in the world, but he still robbed a bank, an act that caused the death of two innocent people. No matter how you look at it, that made him a thief, a bandit. A murderer, an outlaw."

"Names. They're just names people like you tack on anyone who doesn't conform to your set of values."

"Values? Is that what your father taught you about values? That it was right to rob a bank?"

"No, but, you didn't know him like I did. If you could only understand what he was like."

Bolt grabbed a straight-back chair, plunked it down in front of her and sat down.

"I've got nothing but time. If you want to tell me all about how decent your father was, I'll listen."

"No," she said. "He's dead and I'm not going to talk about him."

"Then tell me about the robbery."

"You already know about it."

"Where's the money, Lupita?" he challenged her.

"I won't tell you," she said stubbornly. "You can

85

shoot me like Jose tried to do and I still won't tell you. And I don't even have my gun."

Bolt pulled Lupita's pistol from his waistband and set it on the low table behind him.

"You mind if I take a look at your satchel?" He nodded toward the bag by her feet.

Lupita snatched the carpetbag off the floor, shoved it in his face.

"If you get some sort of a peculiar thrill out of looking at women's undergarments, then go ahead." She settled back in the comfortable chair, folded her hands, and watched him with a smug look on her face.

Damn her, Bolt thought. She knew how to get under a man's skin. In fact, she'd proved that a few minutes before when she'd taunted Jose Contreras.

He set the satchel on his knees, unbuckled the fastener, and opened the leather flap. He pulled it open and glanced inside. On top was the pretty blue dress she'd worn the night before and the scent of it stirred something inside him. He pulled it back and saw the white panties that she'd referred to. He wouldn't give her the satisfaction of knowing that he'd seen them.

He rummaged through the bag, careful not to mess up the carefully folded contents. He knew, even before he did so, that the money would not be there. The bag wasn't nearly heavy enough to be carrying that much money. Nor was it big enough, with all those clothes jammed inside. He fingered some coins he found in the bottom of the bag and brought them out, spread them out across his open palm. There were four five-dollar gold pieces and three coins of lesser value. A little over twenty dollars.

"That's not part of the stolen money, Bolt," Lupita said as she scooted forward in the chair again. "My father gave me that money before the robbery. He wanted me to have it in case anything happened to him." She hesitated a minute. "It was the only money he had in the world."

Bolt glanced over at her when he heard her voice crack with emotion. He didn't know what to make of it. If O'Rourke had only twenty dollars to his name, that could explain why he'd robbed the bank. Maybe he was just a devoted family man, as Lupita had indicated, who was trying to provide for his family. Still, robbing a bank was a crime. It was not a legal way to solve his problems. O'Rourke had taken a gamble, and he'd lost.

Bolt dropped the coins back into her satchel, closed the bag, and buckled the latch. "You'd better take good care of those coins," he said as he scooted the bag back to her. "You may not live long enough to recover the money you stole."

"I didn't steal the money. I rode to Austin with my father and the Mexicans he hired to help him, but I wasn't there when they robbed the bank. My father insisted I stay in the hotel."

Bolt scooted his chair forward until their knees were nearly touching.

"Listen to me, Lupita," he said, trying to reason with her. "If you don't tell where that money is hidden and see that it's returned to the bank, then you're just as guilty as those who did rob the bank. You'll be tracked mercilessly, by lawmen and bounty hunters who won't give a damn that you're a woman. And by the other bandits. It isn't an easy road to take."

"I don't care. I won't tell anybody. I promised my father."

Damned stubborn bitch.

"It's dirty money, Lupita, and it will only cause you

87

grief. Enough blood has been spilled already. If you keep it, there's no doubt in my mind but what you'll die."

"I'll take my chances," she said defiantly.

"Like your father did?"

"Yes. Like my father did."

Bolt was frustrated. Lupita just wouldn't listen to his reasoning.

"How many more will come after you, Lupita? How many more outlaws will track you down and kill you for that money?"

"There are two more *bandidos* besides Pedro Nieves who know I'm alive," she said. "And I know they will come. Nieves is with them by now. I know he is. I know that when Pedro ran away from here during the gunfight, he went to find them."

"Do you know they're in San Antonio?"

"Holed up near there, probably. They think that's where the money is hidden."

"And is it?"

She gave him a dirty look. "I won't tell you, so don't try to trick me."

"Who are the other bandits?"

"Fidel Diamante and Juan Maromero. It is Fidel, *el demoledor*, that I worry about."

"Why?"

"They call him 'The Destroyer.' He is a very bad man. He is the one who killed the teller and the woman. He is ruthless."

"So are you, it seems," Bolt said, his voice full of sarcasm. But he knew there was more to Lupita than she was willing to tell.

Tired of trying to knock some sense into the mestiza's head, he stood up and pushed his chair back. He retrieved her pistol from the low table and shoved it to her, butt first.

"Stay here or leave when you want to," he said. "It doesn't matter to me. You can fight your own damned battles. It's obvious that you don't need me to take care of you."

"Quite obvious," she said with slow, punctuated phrases. "I certainly didn't need you to help me with Jose Contreras. In fact, I didn't even know you were out there. I thought you were too busy with your own pleasure to notice that I was leaving."

"What's that supposed to mean?" he snapped.

"Nothing, Bolt. It just seems that we have different sets of values."

Chapter Eight

Bolt tangled with Tom early the next morning, while they were eating breakfast up at the ranch house.

Bolt had slept in the bordello for what remained of the short night, but not because of Lupita. He'd given up on her, frustrated by her stubbornness. Worried that the other bandits would come in search of the money, he'd stayed in the bordello to protect Harmony and the four harlots. He was up at dawn and had washed up in his room before sitting down to the breakfast Harmony had fixed for them.

"But you can't bury that body on the ranch," Tom argued. He'd been mad when he found out that the mestiza was still there. But with this news, his temper flared. He took a sip of coffee, then slammed the mug down on the table.

"Look, Tom, I promised Lupita I'd bury the Mexican's body here."

"So what do you owe that damned half-breed bitch?" Tom roared.

"Not a damned thing, Tom. You don't really like her, do you? Not like you to turn your nose at a pretty lady." Bolt grinned and it only increased Tom's irritation.

"First of all, she's no lady," Tom said as he jammed his fork into a piece of sausage and stuck it in his mouth. "And hell no, I don't like her. I damned near got my ass shot off last night because of that little hussy."

"You're still here, ain't you?"

"You're harboring a criminal, Bolt, and that's against the law. I don't want no part of it. And don't ask me to dig a grave for that damned bastard."

"I'll get Chet and Rusty to do it, Tom, so relax."

"I still say, take him into town and dump him at the sheriff's office along with the others. And take Lupita with you. She's not our responsibility. She'll be nothing but trouble as long as she's here."

"I can't do that, Tom. If we cart Contreras's body in to the sheriff, sure as hell the other bandits'll get wind of it. They'll be swarming all over the place."

"They'll come anyway. As long as that dirty, thievin' half-breed's here."

"I'll have Rusty and Chet take the body out beyond our property line. Would that make you happy?"

"No, it's still called conspiracy. You're putting your neck in a noose, Bolt, and I ain't gonna be around to watch you swing."

"Tom, can't you have a little patience?"

"Patience, my ass. We ain't gonna get a good night's sleep around here until Lupita's gone."

"I found out a lot last night by talking to Lupita," Bolt said, "and I'm going to get to the bottom of this."

"Did you find out where the money is?" Tom said sarcastically.

"No, not yet. But I will."

"I don't see what your interest is in this whole mess." Tom scooped up a forkful of fried eggs, held it

91

in front of him as he eyed his friend. "Not unless you got some plans for part of the money."

Bolt saw the twinkle in Tom's eyes.

"If I didn't know better, I'd say you was askin' to get your face rearranged. And come to think about it, it might not be a bad idea."

"It'd be better than loosing my balls over a pretty girl," Tom grinned. "Every damned time you get tangled up with a new gal, you end up in a deep barrel of shit. You'd be better off payin' a gal to spread her legs. No strings attached."

"Not when I can get it free," Bolt smiled. "Never."

"Do what you want, Bolt. You will anyway," Tom said as he wiped his napkin across his mouth. "It could take you weeks to untangle this damned mess, and I don't want to even think about the trouble that's comin' our way with that O'Rourke gal hangin' around here."

"Patience, Tom," Bolt grinned as he held his coffee mug up in a toast. "The pot's boiling now. Soon something will flow over the sides."

When Bolt went outside to do his chores, he purposely avoided going near the bordello. Lupita would be scared, he knew, now that the shock of yesterday's gruesome events had had time to sink in. But he had no desire to talk to her. Let her sweat it out on her own.

Lupita slept until noon when Harmony came in to check on her.

"Are you awake, Lupita?" Harmony called as she entered the room.

Lupita stirred, blinked her eyes open, saw the unfamiliar surroundings. Feeling the softness of the

92

featherbed beneath her, and not being accustomed to the luxury of such comfort, it took her a brief time to realize where she was. And then, as she remembered, the pain clawed at her heart, filled her stomach with knots, and caused the nausea to well up in her throat again.

Her father was dead, gone forever, and nothing she could do would bring him back.

If only her father hadn't insisted on robbing the bank. She'd begged him not to, told him that they'd find another way without that money.

If only they could have ridden faster and outdistanced the posse that was tracking them. They knew they were being tracked. They'd spotted the dusty column of riders behind them more than once during the past four days and it had only made her father push on harder.

If only they'd pushed on another night instead of stopping at this ranch. Even though by that time they were all exhausted to the point of dropping, maybe they still could have outrun the posse if they'd tried.

If only her mother . . .

Too many ifs. No solutions. There was no way to bring her father back to life.

"Yes, I'm awake," she said.

"Good," Harmony said. "I'm fixing lunch downstairs. When you're dressed, come down."

"I'm not really hungry," she said as she glanced over at the pretty blonde.

"You need your strength," Harmony said gently. "I'm sorry about your father, Lupita. I truly am. I know how hard it is to lose a loved one, but I also know that your father would want you to take care of yourself."

"Yes, I know he would," Lupita said. "I'll be down

93

in a few minutes."

Lupita sat up on the edge of the bed and watched Harmony go out of the room. She liked the woman. Harmony had been kind to her and she understood why Bolt liked Harmony. She just didn't understand her own jealousy. It was something she'd thought about during the night and it had kept her mind off her father for at least a little while.

Her father's death had upset her more than she wanted to let on, but she had to be brave now. She had to keep her promise to her father.

Lupita hadn't fallen asleep until long after the early light of dawn had filtered into the bedroom that was strange to her. She hadn't slept in a real bed since the night before the bank robbery when they'd stayed at the Austin hotel. After the robbery, her father had come by the hotel to get her. She'd been relieved to see him, and at that time she'd had no inkling of the hard days and nights to follow. They'd ridden for four days and nights, eating only the jerky they carried with them, drinking from canteens that were hard to keep filled because they passed so few streams, sleeping on the hard ground when they'd stopped to rest.

The exhaustion had finally caught up with Lupita, and once she fell asleep she slept deeply for a long time. And now, she had no desire to get up out of the soft bed.

Even at her home in Mexico, she had no soft bed to sleep in. She and her parents lived in a hovel, a shack, just like the other poor families who lived around them. At home, her bed was made from several layers of tattered blankets spread on top of the bare dirt floors. A faded curtain, strung between the corner where she slept and the spot where her parents slept on a similar blanket pad, offered her the only privacy she had.

Lupita and her family had been poor all their lives, but they had been extremely happy, and she hadn't really known how poor they were until she was in her teens, just a few years back.

Lupita spoke English and Spanish with equal ease, although her English still took on an Irish brogue. Even though they lived in Mexico, where they were surrounded by other Mexican families, Lupita had known how to speak English ever since she was born. Her father had wanted better things for his daughter than he'd been able to provide, and he'd insisted that English be the only language spoken in the house. When she was little, she'd learned Spanish from her playmates.

When Lupita was fourteen, her father had sent her to live with his sister in a small town in southern Texas. It was there that Lupita learned that other people slept in beds that were up off the floor. It was there that she learned that the townspeople bought goods from a store instead of making them, that they bought meat in a butcher shop instead of butchering the animals themselves. And it was there that she got her education, by going to school and by reading the hundreds of books her aunt gave her.

After two years with her aunt and uncle, Lupita was not unhappy to go back to Mexico where she once more lived in squalor. She loved her parents very much, and once she was back home she considered her lifestyle to be reality, and the world of her aunt and uncle, a fantasy.

She adored her mother, who was a beautiful, dark-skinned, dark-eyed Mexican named Alicia. She just wished her mother hadn't become so thin and frail these past two years. From the time she was little,

Lupita had wanted to look like her mother, who could have been very elegant if only Lupita's father had had the money to buy her fancy clothes.

But Lupita didn't blame her father for their lack of money. Barney O'Rourke had wanted to move his small family to Texas where there would be more opportunity to earn a decent living. It had been Lupita's mother's choice to remain in Nuevo Laredo, Mexico, where people were poor and wore tattered clothes and no shoes most of the time. Nuevo Laredo, where there was barely enough food to feed the population. They grew all the food they ate, raised all the animals they butchered, and yet there were times when it was not enough.

Lupita stood up and shook her head. It did no good to think about such things. Not now. Not with her father dead, not with knowing that he wouldn't ever be there again when she went home to Nuevo Laredo.

She slipped out of her faded nightgown, which had been patched many times, and put on the only other dress she owned besides the pretty blue one she'd worn the night before. Her aunt had made both dresses.

Lupita smiled then, glad that she'd been wearing the blue dress when her father died in her arms. It was his favorite dress, and when she wore it he had always told her she looked like her mother. The dresses were like new, because she would not wear them at home, where her friends wore tattered clothes.

The frock she put on now was light brown, trimmed with piping that was a darker brown. It was a simple dress, but she wished it was black, under the circumstances.

She finished dressing, brushed her long, flowing hair longer than she needed to. She dreaded going downstairs, where she might run into Bolt. Not that she didn't like him. She did. Probably more than she should. But he would try to pry information out of her and she would have to turn stubborn again and refuse to tell him. She had a promise to keep to her dead father and nothing would keep her from breaking that promise, not even her secret feelings for the man called Bolt.

She knew that Bolt was right about her father's being a thief, even though she hated to admit it. She'd known her father was wrong to get the money that way, and it sickened her that Fidel Diamante had murdered the teller and the innocent woman. But she hadn't been able to talk her father out of it.

Lupita took a deep breath and felt herself weakening. Maybe she'd have to tell Bolt everything, after all. She needed his help, needed someone's help. She knew she'd have to leave the ranch today and be on her way. Bolt wouldn't try to stop her, she was sure of that. She had to dig up the money and carry it with her when she made the hard, lonesome trip back to Nuevo Laredo.

That was what scared her. She knew the other bandits would come looking for her and would kill her if they had to in order to steal the money away from her. She didn't think she could fight them off if they found her. She was good with the gun because her father had taught her to shoot, but she'd been lucky last night when she'd faced Jose Contreras. She knew Jose's weaknesses, his temper, and she knew how to play him along until he exploded. Even before he'd pulled the trigger, she'd known just exactly when he was going to fire.

With Pedro Nieves, Juan Maromero, and especially Fidel Diamante, she knew she wouldn't be so lucky.

97

They were cold-blooded murderers and they would kill her without blinking an eye. She needed someone to ride with her. She needed Bolt's help, but dared not ask for it.

The smell of cooking beef drifted up to her room and made her realize how hungry she was. She walked downstairs, hating the step that creaked, and found Harmony and the four harlots in the large kitchen of the bordello.

"Good morning, Lupita," Doreen said pleasantly.

"Good morning," Lupita said, forcing a smile.

"It's hardly morning," Cathy Boring said. She had red, curly hair, and Lupita noticed the freckles that had been hidden by bright red rouge the night before.

"Did you sleep well?" Linda Ramsey said. She had blond hair and her large breasts didn't spill out of her dress as they had done before. Cathy's dress was high-necked, and although it showed that she had ample breasts, it didn't cling to them.

"Well enough," said Lupita.

"We're sorry about your father," Winny Hart said, and Lupita knew she meant it.

"Thank you."

Lupita felt as if all the girls were staring at her as they sat around the big table. It was as if they didn't know what to say to her. But she soon realized that she was also staring at them.

It surprised her to see that the girls looked freshly scrubbed and wore no makeup this morning. It also surprised her to see that they wore plain, ordinary frocks, more like her own. The night before, the girls had worn tight, low-cut gowns that clung to their bodies. Now they had no bangles or inexpensive jewelry. No bare legs or cleavage showing. No heavy scent of cheap perfume.

Suddenly, Lupita felt awkward, out of place, as she realized that she was actually in a bordello, talking to the real, live soiled doves. The harlots seemed nice enough, but she knew what kind of a reputation such girls had. Loose women, sinful, immoral, looked down upon by society.

And yet, who was she to judge?

In her own way, was she not just as sinful as they? At least, these women hadn't stolen from anyone, as far as she knew. Neither had Lupita, but she knew where the stolen money was and she planned to dig it up and use it for her own purposes. Wasn't that just as bad as actually stealing the money?

"Sit down," Harmony offered as she pulled out an empty chair. "We've been waiting for you."

"You shouldn't have waited," she said as she took a seat. "I'm sorry I slept so long."

"We all slept late," Linda laughed.

"Not Harmony," Cathy said in a catty tone. "She was up at dawn fixing Bolt's breakfast."

"Enough of that, Cathy," Harmony cautioned. "That's what I'm paid for. To fix meals for the boys, scrub their clothes, mend their socks, make their beds, cook for you girls, watch over you, keep you happy."

"You keep Bolt happy, too," Cathy teased.

"You're jealous," Doreen said. "Just because he won't sleep with you."

"He would if I wasn't a whore," Cathy pouted. "He told me so."

"Girls, please," Harmony said. "We have a guest."

Suddenly, Lupita felt more at ease. It struck her funny to be called a guest in a bordello and she almost laughed aloud, something that she hadn't done in a long time. "That's all right," she smiled. "Reminds me of home."

"Do you fight with your sisters?" Harmony asked as she set a platter of roast beef on the table. Doreen and Winny jumped up to help Harmony carry the food.

"No," Lupita said. "I'm an only child. But my friends have sisters and they bicker all the time."

"Where do you live?" Harmony asked.

Lupita felt her muscles tighten up, felt her teeth clench together. Was Harmony trying to pump her for information?

"South of here. I always wanted a sister," she said quickly.

"We're like sisters," Doreen said as she set two bowls on the table, one of mashed potatoes, the other of thick gravy. "We do our share of bickering, as you can see, but we're really very close. We even borrow each other's clothes and jewelry."

Winny brought another two bowls: green beans and tender carrots. "It was a good crop," she smiled as she set the bowls on the table.

"You grow your own food?" Lupita asked.

"Of course, we do," Harmony said proudly as she brought a pitcher of milk to the table and started pouring it in the sparkling tumblers. "And we grow our own milk."

All the girls laughed.

"We have a big garden," Doreen said as she brought pickles and radishes, then took her seat. "And we've put up enough tomatoes and zucchini to last us all year."

"I'm surprised," Lupita said.

"Why?" asked Cathy.

"I just thought . . . well, you know . . . thought all you did was . . . take care of the men."

100

"That's how we earn our wages," Winny said, "but we're just ordinary people. We even make our own clothes."

"It keeps them out of trouble." Harmony winked as she took her place at the table.

And then Lupita asked the two questions she'd wanted to ask since she got there.

"What's it like to be a harlot? What's it like to work for Bolt?"

Chapter Nine

"This is a feast." Lupita said as she took the platter when it was passed. She stuck her fork into a slice of beef and slid it onto her platter, next to the potatoes and gravy. "Do you always eat this well?"

"Yes," Harmony laughed. "We always have plenty of food, and we like to eat our big meal at noon."

Plenty of food. It was something Lupita wasn't used to. She wished there was some way she could take some of the vegetable seeds down to Nuevo Laredo and share them with her parents, her friends. They would need water, too. That was their main problem with growing food.

But her father wasn't there in Nuevo Laredo, she remembered, as the pain stabbed at her heart again. He'd never be there again. It was so hard to accept his sudden death.

"It's a wonder you're not all fat," Lupita smiled.

"We've learned not to take second helpings," Linda laughed.

"Just wait until you taste Harmony's cherry pie," said Doreen.

"Pie, too?" Lupita said.

"I like her chocolate cake better," Cathy said.

Lupita felt totally at ease with these girls as they

shared the meal and friendly conversation. They told her that Bolt paid them a decent salary and protected them from brutal men at all times, didn't force them to sleep with any man they didn't want to.

They told her about the cottages out back, which were kept spotless, where the girls had privacy while they pleasured a man. They explained that they mingled with the customers in the large living room of the bordello, talked to the men there, but never slept with them in the house. That was their home.

It was obvious to Lupita that all of the girls worshiped Bolt, and she realized that he hadn't forced them into that kind of life. Rather, he had tried to discourage them unless he was sure that they wanted to be prostitutes. He didn't hire virgins, because he figured they had a right to discover sex on their own.

The thing that surprised her most was that Bolt refused to sleep with any of the harlots, as Tom did.

"Bolt doesn't believe in mixing business with pleasure," Doreen said. "And I think he's right. I think it could cause a lot of problems if he paid extra attention to one of us girls."

"What about Tom?" Lupita asked.

"Tom's a good friend and fun to be around," Winny said. "Bolt's a friend, too, but he's the businessman." She explained that Tom was not allowed to demand their services, but that if one of the girls wanted to make love to Tom, she did so.

"But not during working hours," Cathy said. "Not unless he wants to pay for it, like everybody else. That's one of Bolt's rules."

One of the girls had explained that Harmony was a friend of Bolt's, not a harlot, and as such, she and Bolt often shared his bed up in the ranch house. But never down in the bordello.

Lupita knew better.

Lupita had Bolt figured all wrong, though. She'd heard Harmony sneak downstairs and had followed her down and listened at the bedroom door, and she'd thought Bolt slept with all of the girls. She thought he could pick and choose, beckon a girl to his bed whenever he had the urge. Evidently Bolt had a lot of respect for the harlots, and it was obvious they had a lot of respect for him.

When the meal was finished, Lupita went back up to her room so that she could make her plans to leave. She thought it best to dig up the money during the night, but she dreaded the thought of riding in the dark with so much cash in her possession. Maybe dawn would be better.

For more than an hour she tried to figure out when would be the best time to leave, but she had trouble concentrating on even the slightest of details. She was intrigued by what the girls had told her about Bolt, and he kept intruding on her thoughts.

Her mind swirled until she felt faint.

The hem of her long skirt trailed across the hardwood floor as she strolled restlessly to the window. She pulled the curtain aside and stared down at the ground where her father had died the night before. She could barely stand to look at it and started to turn away when she saw movement over by the stable. It was Bolt and Tom and they looked like they were repairing the hitch rail.

Pain stabbed at her heart when she saw that her father's black stallion was not tied up there, and she wondered where it was. It was the horse she planned to take with her, not only because it had been her father's, but also because she thought the dark horse would make it harder for anyone to see her at night. She saw that the roans were gone, too, but she didn't care about them.

She watched Bolt as he worked, as he moved about, hammering, testing the boards, stooping down to pick up a dropped nail. He looked so tall and slender, so handsome, the way his clothes fit him just so.

As she stared down at him, she found herself wondering what it would be like to make love to him. A rush of heat flooded the sensitive area between her legs and she didn't understand what was happening to her. It was a prickly feeling that seemed to brush gently across places that had never known such a sensation.

Bolt stood back and looked at his work and Lupita saw the two friends smile at each other, exchange a few words. She wished her window was open so she could hear his deep, strong voice.

Would Bolt be gentle with her, or rough? Gentle, she thought, as she watched him stroke the wood of the repaired hitching rail.

The flush of heat seemed to spread up across her entire body, creep into her cheeks. She wondered if it was because of her embarrassment about what she was thinking, or whether Bolt was doing this to her.

Would he think her too naive for his tastes? He would have to teach her what to do. And then would he think badly of her because she had allowed him to make love to her? Did only bad girls have such feelings about a special man? She didn't know these things. She had only heard talk about them.

Bolt removed his hat, stuck it on a nearby post, then wiped his shirtsleeve across his forehead. He glanced up in her direction and she wondered if he'd seen her. Or if he was even looking for her to be in the window.

She took a step back and to the side so that if he looked again, he wouldn't see her watching him. He didn't look up again.

And then the annoyance came again. Bolt hadn't come over to talk to her that afternoon. He hadn't come to check on her in the morning, either. The girls had told her that. Maybe he was just too busy. It was a big ranch and she was sure there were many chores to do and too few hands to do them.

No, that wasn't it. Bolt was avoiding her. He didn't want to see her. As far as she was concerned, Bolt was a rude, stubborn brute. She didn't need his help. She didn't need him for anything. And she certainly wasn't going to make the first move to try to settle their differences. Let Bolt be the one. Let him come to her. She knew he would. She'd seen that look in his eyes when they stood on the porch last evening.

She jerked the curtains closed with a dramatic flair, whirled around, and marched across the room. And then she didn't know what to do with the rest of the day. She was so frightened that the Mexican bandits would track her down and kill her for the money that she couldn't bring herself to leave now.

Finally, she stretched out on the bed and tried to relax. It was the money that was standing between herself and Bolt, she knew, but there was nothing she could do about it. Some day she hoped he'd understand why it was so important to her, but for now, he had no right to demand that she talk about it.

As she stared up at the ceiling and tried to think of other things, thoughts of Bolt kept drifting in and out of her mind. That special warm feeling flowed between her legs again like a floodtide, causing a damp, tickling, hot, glowing sensation. It was a burning itch she couldn't scratch.

She wanted Bolt so badly that she could barely breathe with the fluttering of her heart. He wouldn't come to her, she thought. He was too damned stubborn. If she wanted him to make love to her, she'd have to be the one to make the first move.

By the time she had primped and strolled down to the stable, Lupita saw that Bolt had his stud bay saddled and tied up to the hitch rail. The reddish-brown horse was big, like her father's stallion, she thought, and she could imagine Bolt riding across the land, his shirt flapping in the breeze as he leaned forward. She saw herself on her father's horse, riding beside Bolt as they made their way to her home in Nuevo Laredo, the hoard of money safely tucked away in her saddlebags. She saw that Bolt's horse was gentle and well groomed, which showed her that he cared.

She didn't see Tom anyplace and was glad to be alone with Bolt. She had come to ask him a very personal favor. She walked up and stood a few feet away from him, watched silently for a minute as he leaned over to cinch the saddle thongs tighter.

"Hello, Bolt," she said.

"Afternoon, ma'am," he said, without looking up.

"I wanted to thank you for putting me up. Or putting up with me," she laughed, trying to take the sting out of his coldness to her. She didn't get the response she wanted.

"You already thanked me, ma'am," he said, still keeping his head low.

"Where's my father's horse?" she asked casually.

"Out in the pasture with the roans. Why? You ready to leave?" He glanced up at her briefly and she thought she saw an expression of relief cross his face.

"Not yet. Where's Tom?"

Again he glanced up at her, stared a little longer, glared a little harder. Did she detect a hint of jealousy in those flashing hazel eyes? She couldn't really tell. He'd make a good poker player, she thought as she tried to read his noncommittal expression.

She asked a few more frivolous questions, which he answered curtly, without bothering to make eye contact. His cold aloofness stabbed at her heart and it was all she could do to hold her head up high as she tried to retain some pride, some dignity. The tears started to come anyway and she turned away, knowing that he wanted her to go away and leave him alone. She took a few slow steps, then whirled around. She'd come for a purpose and she wasn't going to allow him to put her off that way.

With nothing to lose but her pride, she decided to make the big plunge. She shook the wrinkles out of her skirt, brushed her hair back away from her face, and took a deep breath to give her courage. She walked over and stood beside his horse, where he would have to notice her.

"Bolt, I have something very personal to talk to you about." Even though her voice was calm, and even when she spoke, she felt her knees begin to tremble beneath her long skirt.

"I'm listening," he said, without looking up from his stooping position.

"Will you look at me, Bolt?" she demanded as she defiantly clamped her arms into small wings at her sides. "I'm trying to talk to you."

Bolt stood up then and looked directly into her eyes.
"Go ahead. Spit it out."

Spit it out? How unromantic, she thought.

She realized that the way she was standing, she must look like a cold fishwife shrew to him. She let her arms drop to her side, tried to relax the slope of her shoulders, soften her harsh position. Under his direct, penetrating gaze, she felt her courage begin to weaken. She was glad he couldn't see her knees snaking. Glad he couldn't hear the flutter of her fast-pumping heart. She was glad he couldn't feel her

108

suddenly sweaty hands, couldn't tell how dry her mouth had become. She took another deep breath to steady herself, and hoped he hadn't noticed.

"Bolt, will you make love to me?" she asked bluntly, not allowing herself time to change her mind.

"Nope."

Bolt turned away so quickly, she knew he hadn't had time to see the pleading in her eyes, or to understand the sincerity of her question. Her heart sank to her stomach, but she wouldn't allow the tears to form. She hated him, the arrogant beast.

"Why not? Am I not good enough for you?" she said, a flippant tone to her voice.

Bolt didn't answer, didn't glance her way.

"Am I not pretty enough for your fancy tastes?" she taunted. She was toying with him, she knew, just as she'd done with Jose Contreras when she'd wanted to provoke the outlaw's emotions to a boiling point. Her shrewd tactics didn't work with Bolt.

"You're pretty enough." He didn't bother to look back at her when he spoke. Instead, he walked away from her and entered the stable.

Lupita felt like she'd been slapped in the face. The sting was as bad. She felt empty inside, as if a big, invisible buzzard had come down from the skies and snatched her dead heart away. Her knees stopped shaking and seemed to crumble instead. She pulled herself up by the bootstraps, squared her shoulders. She wanted some kind of a response from Bolt. Anything.

Filled with a new surge of determination, she trotted after Bolt, followed him into the stable where it was cool in the shade and darker than it had been outside.

"Is it because you're afraid the harlots will laugh at you?" she asked, trying to keep the sarcasm out of her

109

voice as she stared at his back. "Is that why you won't make love to me?"

"Nope. They don't care what I do." He grabbed the saddlebags from a wooden bench, tossed them over his shoulder and headed back outside.

Lupita followed on his heels, stood as close as she dared as Bolt threw the saddlebags over the rump of his horse.

"Is it because I'm a mestiza? A half-breed?" she asked, and her voice was more subdued.

"Nope. Has nothing to do with it." Bolt crouched down to strap the saddlebags in place.

"Then, take me to your bed. Please," Lupita begged.

"Nope."

Bolt stood up and adjusted the heavy leather pouches. Lupita felt him slipping away from her. She knew he was preparing to leave.

"Bolt, look at me."

Bolt paused, glanced over at her, his hands still up on the saddlebags.

"Why won't you make love to me, Bolt? I thought that's what all men wanted."

"They like to do the asking."

"Am I too bold for you, then? Is that what's wrong, Bolt?"

"Nope." He turned his attention back to his horse, tugged a wrinkle out of the saddle blanket.

"Don't you ever say anything but 'nope'?"

"Yep."

"Damn, you're frustrating, Bolt," she snapped. "Why won't you sleep with me? What's so wrong with me that you refuse to go to bed with me?"

"Reckon you'll have to answer that one yourself."

Lupita turned when she heard the approaching hoofbeats and saw Tom riding toward them. She knew

110

she didn't have much time to convince Bolt of her needs.

"It's the money, isn't it?" she said in an accusing manner.

Bolt didn't answer.

She turned sweet and coy, then.

"If I tell you where the money is, will you sleep with me?"

"No," Bolt said firmly. "And you wouldn't anyway, would you?"

"Tell or sleep with you?"

"Both."

"I would sleep with you. That's what I've been trying to tell you," she said with frustration. "Or are you one of those men who does not sleep with women?" she added sarcastically as Tom rode up to them.

Bolt glared at her, but didn't answer. He snatched his Stetson from the post, jammed it on his head, then stuck the toe of his boot into the stirrup and mounted his horse.

"You're leaving now?" Tom asked his friend.

"Yeah," Bolt answered. "There's a chance I won't be back until morning. Can you handle things around here until I get back?"

"I always do, don't I?"

"Yeah, but I mean handle them right," Bolt grinned.

Lupita stared up at Bolt's jovial face and wondered why he couldn't have been that easygoing with her instead of treating her like she was some kind of a bug to be squashed under his boot and then pitched to the winds.

Bolt took the reins in his hand, squared the Stetson on his head. He looked down at her, held her gaze for a moment before he spoke.

111

"Look, Lupita, you're a nice girl, I'm sure, in your own way," he said with a gentle firmness to his voice. "We just don't see eye to eye about what's right and wrong. Let it go at that."

Bolt touched his boot heels to the horse's sides, flipped the reins. The animal responded to his gentle nudge, and before Lupita could speak, Bolt rode away and headed for the road.

Lupita stood there and watched him go. Patches of sunlight danced through the shadows on Bolt's back as he rode slowly along the tree-lined path that led away from her, away from the ranch. She saw how tall and straight he sat in the saddle and wanted him more desperately than she'd wanted him before. She wished she were going with him. More than that, she wished he were going with her.

She batted back the tears that formed in her eyes and turned to Tom, who was still sitting his horse.

"Where is he going?" she asked.

"To town."

"San Antonio?"

"Yair. It's the only town around here."

"What's he going to do there?"

"I don't know," Tom said as he shrugged his shoulders. "He didn't say and I didn't ask."

Lupita knew that Tom wasn't being curt with her, the way Bolt had been.

"Does he have a woman in town?" she asked, hoping she sounded casual.

"Oh, several, I imagine," Tom smiled.

Pangs of jealousy stabbed at her heart. She felt the rush of anger flare up and redden her cheeks.

Without another word, she turned and stalked across the yard. Inside the bordello, she walked right on by the girls who were sitting in the living room. They called to her but she didn't answer. She marched up the stairs to her temporary bedroom, not caring that the girls were staring at her.

In the bedroom, she threw herself down on the bed, buried her head in the pillow, and let the tears come.

She wanted Bolt so much she ached from the desire.

But, right now, the money was more important to her.

Chapter Ten

When he got to the road, he almost turned back.

Bolt hated to leave Lupita that way, hurting like that. He'd seen the sadness in her eyes. If he only had more time to talk to her now, to explain that it was because of her that he was going to town. He wanted to put a stop to this thing before those other three bandits came to the ranch looking for her. He didn't want anymore bloodshed on his property. And since Lupita refused to give up the money, or even tell him where it was, he had no choice but to do some investigating on his own.

Time was precious and he didn't want to spend any more of it trying to get her to tell him the things he needed to know in order to help her. He'd already tried that and it hadn't worked.

He paused only briefly at the spot where his property ended, where the tree-lined path met the main dirt road that led north to San Antonio and south to Pleasanton. Way farther south was the Mexican border.

The heavy wooden sign that marked the entrance to his ranch was tacked to a thick post, easy to read from the road. Large white letters, neatly printed, spelled out the words: ROCKING BAR RANCH. Near the bottom of the sign were their names: BOLT and PENROD, printed in smaller white letters. And under that, in still smaller letters, was a single word: OWNERS. A second sign, not quite as big, was tacked beneath it and carried the legend: ROCKING BED BORDELLO. Bolt noticed that the paint on the weathered signs was faded and, in some spots, had begun to flake off. He made a mental note to repaint the signs, and promised himself he'd do it as soon as he fixed the squeaky step.

He reined Nick to the north, headed toward town, glad to have his faithful horse under him. Nick and Bolt had been riding together for a long time and the animal was sensitive to Bolt's body movements, his voice, his commands. The horse could turn on a dime, responded to the slightest pressure of Bolt's knee against his ribs, came when Bolt whistled for him, and there weren't too many things that spooked him. Not if you didn't count rattlesnakes. Nick never complained, and he'd listen for hours if Bolt felt like talking. There wasn't much more a man could ask of his horse.

Although he didn't have much to go on, Bolt did have the names of the three Mexican outlaws who would kill to get their hands on the money; already had. He knew that the money was buried somewhere around San Antonio. At least, that's what Jose Contreras had said before Lupita had killed him. But Bolt's purpose for going to San Antonio was not to search for the money. He just wanted to find the outlaws and get them behind bars before there was more trouble at the ranch.

The rest was up to Lupita and the law. If he could convince her to turn over the money to the proper authorities, he was sure that no charges would be filed against her. If she refused to do it, she faced a life of hell, even if the outlaws were behind bars.

He let Nick have his head, and after an initial burst of speed Bolt slowed the stud down to a steady pace. In this heat, he didn't want to push the horse. The scorching sun was off to his left, halfway down in the sky. He tilted his hat to keep his face in the shade and unbuttoned his shirt, letting it flap in the breeze to cool him, grateful that there was a breeze. As he rode the two miles to town, Bolt kept his ears and eyes alert for signs of the bandits.

He tried to keep his thoughts on the things he had to do in town, the places he'd go to ask questions, but thoughts of Lupita kept popping into his mind. He saw her as a selfish, greedy hussy, a criminal, who was putting all of them at the ranch in jeopardy by her stubborn refusal to turn the money over. He wanted her to leave the ranch so they could get back to a normal life without fear. He wanted to forget that he'd ever met her. And yet, he was drawn to her, fascinated by the many complicated facets of her personality.

He'd been stunned when she'd come out to the stable and asked him to sleep with her. Under different circumstances, he probably would have carried her up to the house and taken advantage of her offer. As it was, he had difficulty keeping his eyes off of her. If she only knew how much she'd excited him with that look of raw desire in her eyes. It had taken every ounce of will power he had to turn her down.

As he neared town, he forgot about Lupita and concentrated on the things he had to do.

His first stop was the Drift In Saloon, so named, they told him, because most of the customers were drifters. Drifters who never seemed to find work and never had enough money to drink, but drank anyway. Hardcases who thought it was the thing to do to start a fight after they'd gotten a snootful of rotgut whiskey.

Outlaws fresh off the owlhoot trail, stinky and dirty, and trying to stay one jump ahead of the law. These were the kind of raucous, hard-hearted men who drank at the Drift In Saloon.

It was the roughest place in town, and with its reputation for at least one fight enough, the most dangerous. It was a place that Bolt would not enter unless he had a damned good reason. And he had a reason this late afternoon. It was the kind of watering hole that attracted men like the ones he was looking for. He'd been there a few times before and always made it worth the barkeep's time to answer some questions.

He dismounted, hitched Nick to the rail, walked across the wooden planks that were in front of the saloon. The stench of stale beer and spilled whiskey drifted out of the saloon and stung his nostrils, even though the mustiness of sour urine was all around him from places where men had stepped outside to take a leak.

He pushed through the batwing doors, paused long enough to look around. This time of day, there were not more than a dozen men in the bar, and none of them were Mexicans. He went on in and heard the batwing doors swing on rusty hinges behind him. Nobody bothered to look up and he headed straight for the bar.

"Quite a party you had at your spread last night," said Joe, the tall, stoop-shouldered barkeep who stood in front of Bolt. "Everybody was talkin' about it after they brought them bodies to town."

"I wouldn't want to do it again," Bolt said dryly.

"What'll it be?" asked Joe as he took a swipe at the counter with a grimy towel.

"Beer," Bolt said, "I've tasted your rotgut before."

"Got a good batch this time. Not so much tobacco

117

in it and the chili pepper adds some spice."

Bolt knew that Joe tossed anything he had on hand in the pot when he made the brew. It was a way to keep the prices down for the men who drank there.

"Ten cents," Joe said a minute later when he plunked the mug of warm beer in front of Bolt. "Who you looking for this time?"

Bolt smiled at the man. He fished three coins out of his pocket, slid it across the countertop.

Joe grinned when he saw the money. He picked it up with gnarled fingers and tossed it in a tin box under the counter. "Must be somebody important this time," he said.

"Three Mexican outlaws," Bolt said as he sipped from the smudged mug. "You seen 'em."

"Hell, look around," Joe gestured. "Most of the fellows in here are outlaws. They ain't no Mexes in here now, but they's plenty of 'em who come around. You give me a hard one this time."

"Pedro Nieves, Fidel Diamante, Juan Maromero." Bolt rattled off the names. "Ring any bells?"

"Naw. I ain't much good on names."

"They're new in town. Rode in yesterday about noon, near as I can tell."

Joe scratched his balding head.

"I might know who you're talkin' about. Three Mexes came in here yestiddy. Middle of the afternoon, near as I can recall. They belted down a few quick drinks and then left."

"You seen 'em since?" Bolt asked, remembering that Conreras had said that he and his friends were drinking when the bodies were brought into town.

"Yair. A couple of times since," Joe said.

"What were they drinking?"

"Mescal, same as most of the Mexes drink," Joe laughed, not self-conscious about the gaps in his mouth where teeth were missing.

"It figures."

"Were they in here when the bodies were delivered to the sheriff?"

"Yair, they was here. Everybody went out in the street for a while to watch the excitement, but them three Mexes came back in with the rest of 'em. It was wild in here after that." Joe scratched his head again. "I remember now, one of the Mexes left shortly after that and I ain't seen him since."

"Sounds like the ones I'm looking for. You seen the other two today?"

"Yair. Twice. Once early this mornin' and again about noon," Joe said. "Funny thing, though. They was three Mexes come in about dawn this mornin', hungover as hell. I was cleanin' up in here and didn't pay no attention to 'em, 'cept to give 'em their drinks. But when I served 'em their second drinks, I seen that they wasn't the same ones who come in last night."

"What do you mean?"

"Well, two of the Mexes was the same ones, but the other one, he was somebody different."

"Hmmm." Bolt shifted his weight to the other foot.

"The new one must've gotten himself all tangled up in a terrible fight."

"What makes you think so?"

"I seen the big bulge under his shirt. Sure enough, he had a big, thick bandage wrapped around that shoulder of his. I seen the stain on his shirt where the blood leaked through. Left shoulder, I think it was." Joe put his hand to his own right shoulder, then switched it to the left one. "Yep, it were his left shoulder."

"Pedro Nieves," Bolt muttered as he smiled to himself. It had been a damned good shot in the dark. "Were any of the Mexicans riding roans?"

119

"Yeah, they was when they come in this mornin'. I was by myself, sweepin' the floor, and I seen 'em ride up. Don't see how them Mexes can drink like that and still come back for more." Joe shook his head. "That much mescal would probably kill me or you."

"Probably. So, they came back at noon. Right?"

"Yair, and I think they'd been out diggin' for that missin' bank money. They was dirty enough. The talk around town is that the bank robbers got away with fifty thousand dollars. I reckon there'll be a lot of folks out there roamin' around the land, tryin' to find that money."

"I reckon so." Bolt had the answers to some of his questions, at least. "Thanks for your help, Joe. If you see those Mexicans again, make sure the sheriff knows right away."

"Why? You think they had something to do with the robbery?"

"Maybe."

"You mean that them Mexes is bank robbers?"

"Could be."

"Jeez. And to think I was here all alone with 'em this mornin'. I could've been killed."

"Don't worry, Joe," Bolt grinned. "They're after the big money. They wouldn't waste their bullets to get what little cash you've got."

"I reckon that's the truth," Joe laughed.

Bolt left the Drift In Saloon and made his way down the main street of town, stopping at almost every building long enough to go inside and ask questions.

He got the same story every time he talked to someone who had seen the outlaws. It seemed that the three Mexicans were like smoke, disappearing into thin air. People had seen them riding along the street, yes, but nobody had noticed them leave. Nobody had seen them come back.

By the time he'd worked his way down to the Mercantile Store at the other end of the long street it was getting dark, and he didn't know much more than when he'd left the Drift In Saloon. He'd learned that the Mexican bandits hadn't eaten in any of the few cafes in town, hadn't stayed in the hotels.

His spirits sagged. He was running out of places to look. When he was through at the Mercantile Store, he'd ride over to Dr. Parmenter's office, which was at his home on the next street over. But he was saving that for last, hoping for an invite to stay for dinner. He wanted to talk to August Parmenter, find out if the bandit had been there, but the main reason was he wanted to spend some time with the doctor's beautiful daughter, Hallie Dumont.

As he tied Nick to a hitching post in front of the store, he hoped Hallie was still there. She was a widow, a beautiful southern belle. Her late husband, Bill Dumont, had been part owner of the Mercantile Store, along with Charlie Anderson. When Bill had died of a ruptured appendix just three short months ago, Hallie had taken over her husband's interest in the Mercantile Store.

He strolled across the boardwalk and thought about how he and Hallie had become such good friends since her husband's death. They had spent a lot of pleasant Sunday afternoons together, but hadn't been lovers. He'd wanted her enough times, but had thought it too soon to ask.

He entered the store and glanced around, didn't see Hallie, thought maybe she was in the storeroom at the back of the cluttered store.

"Howdy, Bolt," Charlie Anderson said. "Seems you had yourself a time of it last night. Glad none of you got hurt."

"Thanks, Charlie. Is Hallie still here?"

"Nope. You missed her by half an hour. You've taken a fancy to her, haven't you?"

"She's a pretty girl, Charlie. What man wouldn't be taken with her?" Bolt grinned.

"If you ask me, I think she's smitten with you, too." Charlie gave Bolt a knowing smile. "I've seen the way she looks at you when you come in."

"Wouldn't surprise me none. I ain't bad lookin'," Bolt teased. "I'll bet you've got your own moments of sinful thoughts when she's around, you old buzzard."

"At my age?" Charlie laughed as he patted his gray head. "Hell, all I got left is my sinful thoughts and I don't see no harm in thinkin' them."

"That's the way to look at it. I'm looking for those bank robbers. Three Mexicans. Have you seen them?"

"There've been several Mexicans in here today, but I couldn't say that any of them looked like bank robbers. Besides, none of them came in sets of three." The wrinkles in Charlie's forehead deepened as he tried to think. "What do bank robbers look like, anyway?"

"I don't know," Bolt laughed.

"Maybe they should wear a goddamned sign around their necks so we'd recognize them."

"You're a big help, Charlie."

"I try to be. Can I sell you anything while you're here?"

"Always got your hand out, don't you, Charlie? You're nothing but a greedy shopkeeper, you know that?"

"Keeps the bread buttered. I'll bet if Hallie was here, you'd find something to buy."

"Yeah, and I'd take my damned sweet time buying it, too, just so I could look at her pretty face. You ever think about that, Charlie? If you had a face like hers, you'd sell ten times as much as you do now."

"With this old body?" Charlie said as he patted his fat belly. "It'd look silly on me."

"I'd like to sit around and chew the fat, but I've gotta go."

"I know where you're going, too. You're heading straight over to Hallie's house, where you're gonna try to wangle an invite to dinner."

"You hit it on the head, Charlie. That's just where I'm going."

"Hope she serves you up something nice and sweet after dinner." Charlie winked.

"You dirty old lecher." Bolt snatched his Stetson off, took a playful mock swing at the old man's face, missed by inches. "I've got to go before I miss dinner."

Bolt slid his Stetson back into place, turned, and started for the door.

"Oh, by the way, Bolt," Charlie called. "Did those two fellows find your ranch all right?"

Bolt turned back toward the old man.

"What two fellows?"

"The ones who were asking about you this morning."

An alarm sounded in Bolt's mind. He walked closer to Charlie.

"Who were they?" he asked.

"I don't know." Charlie shrugged his shoulders. "A couple of Mexican fellows. Didn't ask their names. Wouldn't have remembered them if I had."

"What'd they want?" Bolt asked, his heart suddenly pounding in his chest.

"Shovels," said Charlie. "They came to buy a couple of shovels. Hell, they were camped out on my doorstep when I came to work this morning, just waitin' for me to open up. Smelled like they'd been up drinkin' all night. The fumes damned near brought me to my knees," he laughed.

"Dammit, Charlie, I mean why were they asking for me?" Bolt snapped.

"Don't know why. They just wanted directions to your ranch."

"Did you tell 'em?"

"Yep. Figured they were lookin' to hire on as ranch hands."

Bolt raged with fury.

"I ain't hiring," he said, a cold, hard edge to his words. He turned and marched toward the door.

"Hell, don't go getting testy with me," the old man shouted after him. "The location of your Rocking Bar Ranch is no big, fat secret around these parts. Anybody in town would have told those fellows where you lived."

"Shit!" Bolt said in frustration. It didn't matter, anyway. If Pedro Nieves had hooked up with the other two by now, he could show them where to go.

"Maybe if you didn't have a whorehouse out there," Charlie said without malice, "you could lead a nice secluded life, if that's what you want. But havin' them girls out there is an open invitation to strangers."

"You're right, Charlie. Didn't mean to jump down your throat."

"Don't bother me none. And if those bastards come back, I'll blow their damned lights out for you."

"Thanks, Charlie, you lecherous old shopkeeper."

"Enjoy your dessert."

Bolt walked out of the Mercantile Store and a hard knot formed in the pit of his stomach. He was sick to think that the bandits knew where he lived. Sicker still, that they wanted to know.

Chapter Eleven

Hallie Dumont answered the door and threw her arms around Bolt, hugged him tight.

The sudden warmth of her body, the crush of her firm breasts against his chest, caused his manhood to dance and begin to grow. Never before had he seen such a show of affection from Hallie, who was usually more timid, more proper. They had held hands a few times in the past couple of weeks, even shared a few kisses, but it had never gone beyond that.

She let him go and stood back.

"Oh, Bolt I was so worried about you when I learned about the trouble you had at the ranch last night. What a terrible thing to happen."

Bolt caught his breath, looked down at the beautiful blonde. Even after working at the store all day, she looked fresh and clean, smelled like she'd just stepped out of a bouquet of spring flowers.

"Not to worry," he smiled, using one of her favorite expressions. "You look lovely tonight, Hallie. As you always do. A vision in blue, purer than any sky."

"Why, I declare, Mr. Bolt, I do believe you're flirting with me." She batted her eyelashes, a teasing flicker in her bright blue eyes.

"And I'd say it was the other way around."

Her laughter had a musical tinkle to it. It was one of the many things he liked about Hallie. Just the sound of it could melt his insides.

"I do believe you're right," she said, dipping her head down in mock shyness. And then she raised her head and sighed. "I'm really glad to see you."

"The pleasure is mine, as always," he said and removed his hat. "Is your father home, Hallie?"

"Oh, yes. Forgive me," she said, stepping aside. "Please come in."

"Thank you."

Bolt had been there before. He liked the comfortable house and wondered at Hallie's ability to keep it so clean when she worked all day. Her father's medical treatment room, which was beyond the living room and off to the left, always smelled of ointments, but Hallie managed to keep the sickly-sweet odor from the rest of the house.

The hand-painted vase on the small entrance table always held a fresh bouquet of flowers, when they were in season. The scent in the vestibule this time was a delicate mingling of lavender and honeysuckle.

"He's in his office," she said.

"Thanks. I'll find my way."

"Bolt, you will stay for supper won't you? I'm fixing chicken and dumplings."

"I was hoping you'd ask. Smells delicious."

"It's almost ready, so please tell Father that he can only take up ten minutes of your time. I'll expect both of you to be at the table promptly."

"Yes, ma'am."

"Do you plan to stay in town tonight?" she asked.

"I don't know yet."

"Well, just remember that we have a spare bedroom here and you're welcome to stay if you don't wish to ride home before morning."

"Thanks. I may take you up on it."

With that, Hallie turned and walked away.

Dr. August Parmenter glanced up from his book when Bolt knocked at the open door. The treatment room was just down the hall.

"Oh, come in, Bolt. I was just thinking about you. I heard the news about the shootout and I'm glad none of your people got hurt."

Bolt liked the doctor's easy manner and he always enjoyed talking to him. Parmenter was tall and slender, dark-haired, distinguished looking with the touch of gray at his temples.

"So am I."

"Please sit down, Bolt."

Bolt sat in the padded straight chair across from the doctor's desk, stretched his legs out in front of him.

"Did you treat a Mexican man for a bullet wound some time today?"

Parmenter looked surprised. "As a matter of fact, I did. Early this morning. Sometime before dawn. How did you know?"

"One of the bank robbers got away last night. I took a wild shot at him in the dark as he was fleeing on horseback. I heard him groan, but I wasn't sure I'd hit him. It must be the same one you treated."

"Oh, if I'd only known," Parmenter said as he leaned forward in his chair.

"You would have treated him anyway."

"Yes, of course. But I would certainly have notified the authorities after I was finished. He told me that he'd just ridden in from the north, and that he'd been attacked during the night and robbed of most of his

127

money and then shot and left to die on the road. It didn't dawn on me to connect him to the gun battle out at your ranch."

"I just hope he paid you for your services."

"Yes, he did. Said his name was Roberto Garcia."

"As phony as a John Smith," Bolt smiled. "How bad did I nick him?"

"Considering the fact that you were shooting blind, it was a pretty fair shot. You caught him in the left shoulder. Six inches lower and a little to the left, and you would have hit his heart.

"Is he very bad? Is he too sick to ride?"

"He was in a lot of pain when he got here. He'd lost a lot of blood so he was pretty weak. I removed the bullet and bandaged the wound when I was finished. But he's certainly in no condition to ride. Not yet, anyway."

"How long will it be before he can ride again?"

"A couple of days. He'll be sore for a long time, but I think he could safely ride in two days without causing any problems."

"That might buy me some time," Bolt said.

"I wouldn't count on it, Bolt. I tried to convince him to stay in one of our rooms for a day or two so that I could check for infection and change his bandages. But darned if he didn't get up and ride away on his horse."

"He came alone, then?"

"Yes. He said he didn't have very far to ride. He told me that he had to meet some friends who would take care of him. I advised him against moving for at least twenty-four hours, but there was no way I could keep him here against his will."

"No, but I think I know who his friends are. Fidel Diamonte and Juan Maromero."

"You know them?" Dr. Parmenter asked.

128

"I know of them, that's all. From what I know, Diamonte and Maromero were with Pedro Nieves and the others when the bank was robbed."

"And they're still alive?"

"Yes," Bolt said as he shook his head.

"The report I heard was that all the bank robbers were dead. I didn't know."

"There's something else you don't know," Bolt said. "I need to tell you something in confidence." He sat up taller in his chair, leaned forward.

"Everything you say to me in this room is held in confidence, Bolt, unless you tell me otherwise."

"I know. The leader of the band was an Irishman named O'Rourke. Barney O'Rourke. Besides the three Mexicans I'm trying to track down, there's another survivor of the robbery, and I don't want anybody to know about it just yet. Not even the sheriff.

"Oh?" Parmenter's eyes widened slightly.

Bolt picked up a pencil from the desktop, twirled it in his fingers.

"Yes. O'Rourke had a daughter named Lupita. She wasn't in on the bank robbery, but she rode with her father and the Mexicans before and after the money was stolen. She knew what they were planning all along."

"And where is this Lupita now?" Parmenter raised his hand in the air. "Ah, don't tell me, Bolt. She's out at your ranch."

"Yes, but no one must know."

The doctor leaned back against his chair, stroked his chin.

"You've got yourself in a fine kettle of fish this time, haven't you Bolt?"

"That's not the worst part of it, August," Bolt said as he looked into the doctor's eyes. "Lupita O'Rourke is the only one who knows where the money is buried, and I can't convince her to give it up."

"It's not your responsibility, Bolt. Why don't you turn her over to Sheriff Rankin?"

"Because I think she'd spend the rest of her life behind bars. She's too damned stubborn to tell where the money's hidden. Besides, I think there's more to this whole thing than she'll tell me."

"Has she got any family besides her father?"

"Her mother's living, but if Lupita tried to go home to her, she'd never make it alive. Those three bastard bandits will cut her apart inch by inch until she tells them where the money is hidden. And then, they'll leave her for buzzard bait."

Parmenter sat forward again, stared into Bolt's eyes, a stern, fatherly expression on his face. He spoke in slow, deliberate words. "So you're trying to be the big hero who protects the heroine and kills the villains."

"It isn't like that, August." Bolt's his voice raised slightly, his anger triggered. "I'm not trying to run the whole show by myself. I don't want any shiny stars on my damned grave when I die."

"I understand," Parmenter said, a trace of a smile at the corner of his mouth. "You thought you wanted my advice when you came in here a little while ago. But that's not what you wanted. You just needed a place to sort out your mind."

"I've got three choices don't I, August?" Bolt said, trying to read Parmenter's mind.

"You've got all the choices you want, Bolt."

"Yair. I can turn Lupita over to Sheriff Rankin, which would be the most logical choice. Or I could tell her to leave the ranch, throw her to the wolves, as it were, and let her take her chances."

"Or?" Parmenter prompted.

"Or, I can keep her there at the ranch and protect her until I'm sure the bandits won't get to her."

"Even then, your dilemma won't be solved until the money is in the proper hands."

Bolt shook his head.

The tinkle of a clanging bell rang throughout the house.

"Oh, no," Bolt said. He slapped his fingers across his forehead.

"What's the matter?" Parmenter asked as he rose from his comfortable chair.

"I forgot to tell you that Hallie said supper would be on the table in ten minutes."

"She just told me," Parmenter laughed. He walked around the table and put his arm around Bolt. "And if we don't get in there, we're likely to go to bed without our supper."

"Thanks for your help, doctor," Bolt said as they walked out of the office.

"I didn't do anything but listen."

"That's just what I needed. You helped me make a decision."

"I won't ask which choice you made."

"I don't think you need to," Bolt grinned. "I think you already know what I've decided to do."

"If you need a bed to sleep in tonight, you're welcome to stay here," Parmenter said as the two men walked into the dining room.

"I already invited him, Father," Hallie said.

Bolt saw the suggestive twinkle in her eyes.

He hoped her father hadn't.

"Don't you two ever stop talking?" Hallie said as she joined the men on the back porch after supper. She had already washed and dried the dishes, set

131

them away in the cupboard, and put a fresh dab of perfume behind each ear. "You're worse than two clucking hens."

Bolt looked over at her and smiled, smelled her fresh scent from across the porch where he sat on a wooden bench, the seat cushioned by pillows that Hallie had made. The light of the moon accented the curves of her form-fitting gown, made the shadowy places seem even more secretive, more inviting.

Bolt liked this homey porch, with its fragrant flower bed all around. The wooden chairs and sitting bench glistened in the moonlight, and the cushions that Hallie had sewn made the furniture easier to sit on. This porch was where he and Hallie had spent many pleasant evenings, talking in the moonlight, laughing as they watched the fireflies in the field, trying to pick the exact spot where the next one would flash its beacon light. The constant hum of the crickets shut off the noise of the town. The house was set so far away from the main street that they usually didn't hear the sounds anyway. Sitting on the back porch made it seem as if they were secluded from the rest of the world.

"You're right, Hallie," Parmenter told his daughter. "It's getting late and I've taken up entirely too much of Bolt's time. It's time for me to retire." The doctor rose from his cushioned chair and said a quick goodnight.

When Hallie's father was gone, Bolt felt a flood of warmth wash over his body, as if a mischievous breeze had stored up the day's heat and chosen this particular time to dump its load on him. It was always like this when he was alone with Hallie.

He ambled over to the porch rail and stared up at the night sky, drank in the coolness of the night. The stars shimmered like a thousand diamonds dancing on

132

a black velvet cloth.

"I'm glad you stayed," Hallie said as she drifted over and stood beside him. She gazed up at the same jewel-studded sky.

He turned his head to look at her and felt heady from the scent of her perfume. In the moonlight she looked like a silver siren, beckoning the sailors to come. Again he felt the warmth, as if tiny sparks of electricity were bouncing back and forth between them.

"Why?" he asked, teasing her with his smile.

"You know why, Bolt," she cooed. "You shouldn't have to ask."

Unable to resist her soft lips, he tipped his head and gave her a brief kiss. As he moved his head back, her lips followed his, wanting more. He faced her then and drew her into his arms, planting his slightly open mouth full on hers. Her body melted into his and he felt the crush of her ample breasts, the thrust of her loins against his.

His manhood began to harden, push against the crotch of his trousers. He backed his lips away, drew in a deep breath, tried to keep from getting any more aroused from her closeness. He didn't have a right to take advantage of her loneliness.

She kissed him again, drawing him to her as if she were magnetized.

"That is one of the reasons I'm glad you stayed," she said, a velvet husk to her voice. "Your kisses feel so good to me."

"And what are the other reasons?" he smiled. With his arms still wrapped around her, he backed away slightly, not trusting himself to be that close.

"You will have to learn them for yourself." Her eyes teased him with their twinkle.

She thrust her warm, supple body against him

133

again, kissed him full on the mouth. He felt the damp warmth of her lips, the burning pressure of her loins against his own. He slid his tongue inside her mouth, flicked it across her responding tongue, wishing he were plumbing her other depths.

His hands slid slowly down her back, applying a gentle pressure that drew her pliable body nearer. When his hands reached her hips, he pulled her tight against him. His heart pounded with desire. His mind blotted out everything else.

He let her go suddenly, leaned away from her to catch his breath, to stabilize his rocketing emotions.

"Why do you keep backing away from me?" she teased. "Do you not find me desirable?"

"Oh, Hallie, I find you too desirable," he said, a deep, raspy husk in his voice.

"When will you make love to me, Bolt?" she said. "I cannot wait much longer."

"We can't, Hallie. Not yet."

"Why can't we? We have the same burning desires. We are old enough to know what we want."

"But you're so recently widowed."

"Widows need to be loved, too," she said. "Just because my husband is dead doesn't mean that my desires died with him."

"But, Hallie, it has been such a short time since your husband died. It has been only three short months."

"Three months can be a long time. It depends on how you look at it. For me, it has been much too long."

"There should be a proper time of mourning, shouldn't there?"

"Who told you that?" Her eyes flared with a sudden anger.

"Society dictates it, I guess. It's just one of those

things that everybody understands."

"I don't understand it," she hissed. "How long does society say I must wait to be fulfilled again? A year? Two years? Would that be proper? Five? For some, I'm sure, ten years would not be enough time to wait."

"You're right," he said.

"It is my life, Bolt, and this thing you call society has no right to tell me when I can be happy and when I cannot. It has no right to put a time period on my mourning. I carry my grief for my dead husband in my heart, and it will always be there for him. But it has nothing to do with the way I feel about you."

"I understand, Hallie," he said gently.

"Do you? I wonder."

"I think I do."

"Unless you have been in such a situation, you cannot know what it is like. You cannot feel the pain, the loneliness, of being forced to love only something that is already dead."

Bolt stared into her eyes and saw the hurt.

"Were you and your husband happy?" he asked.

"Yes, very," she said. "He gave me much pleasure in our bed, if that's what you mean."

"Then how can you think of making love to another man so soon after his death?"

"Bolt, it is *because* Bill and I were happy in our lovemaking that I want another man. If he had been mean or cruel to me, or rough with me in bed, or unfeeling when he made love to me, then I would probably never want to make love again. Such a relationship would have left me with bad feelings about sex. But it was a good thing we had together, and I have those same desires now. I wish you could understand."

"I do understand, Hallie. I really do." Bolt drew

135

her close against his body again, and kissed her long and deep, this time with no reservations.

When they finally came up for air sometime later, Hallie asked her question again.

"When will you make love to me, Bolt? I cannot wait much longer."

"How about right now?"

Chapter Twelve

She took him by the hand, led him to her bedroom
at the back of the house.

"But your father will know," Bolt said when they
were inside the room and Hallie had closed the door.

"He doesn't mind," she said. "He likes you."

"He'll hear us."

"No. His bedroom is in the far corner of the house.
We need not make much noise with our love."

"But, still . . ."

"Yes, be still," she whispered as she put her fingers
to his mouth. "You use your mouth for talking, when
there are better things to do with it." She kissed each
corner of his mouth, and once in the middle. "See?"

Bolt had never been in Hallie's bedroom before. It
didn't surprise him to see that it was neat and clean.
The light from a coal-oil lamp, its wick turned down
low, flickered across the room from the dresser. The
rest of the house was decorated with tans and browns,
masculine woods and leather. Hallie's room was feminine, with pinks and shades of purple, frilly curtains
and bedspread. A velvet lavender-colored chair sat
near a low white marble table on one side of the room.
The table held a bouquet of freshly cut flowers, and
some needlepoint work that had been set aside. A

137

writing desk sat in a corner, accompanied by a velvet-cushioned chair.

"Hallie, you are so bold."

"Too bold for your tastes?"

"No," he smiled. "Just bold enough."

He saw that the covers had been turned back and wondered if it had been done for him.

She tugged on his hand, pulled him over closer to her bed. They gazed at each other and then he took her in his arms. Their kiss was full and long as they pressed together, exploring each other with only their thrusting bodies.

It was Hallie who broke the kiss this time.

"Hurry, Bolt," she said as she began to fumble with the buttons at his shirt. "My need is great."

"Are you sure you want me, Hallie?"

"Yes," she husked. "I want you more than anything in the world." She managed to undo two of his buttons before she stopped and started on her own. Bolt removed his gunbelt, hung it over the bedpost. He tugged his shirttail out of the waistline of his pants, finished unbuttoning it. He quickly removed it and let it drop to the floor. He sat down on the edge of the bed to remove his boots. Hallie, her dress partially unbuttoned, sat down beside him and slipped out of her shoes.

Before they stood up again, she leaned over and gave him a brief kiss.

"I want you," she whispered.

"I want you, too," he said.

They stood face to face, watching each other undress. Hallie pushed her dress off her shoulders, tugged it down over her flared hips. The gown slid to the floor and she stepped out of it and stood before him in a lace camisole and white panties.

138

"Hurry," she said again.

Bolt slipped out of his trousers, tossed them to the floor. When he removed his undershorts and stood before her, stark naked, he saw her eyes dart to his crotch.

"You are ready for me," she said.

"Yes. I have been for a long time."

She pulled the camisole over her head, tossed it aside.

Bolt stared as she hooked her thumbs into the band of her panties and pushed them down.

She tilted her head up and waited for his kiss. When he bent to kiss her, he found her mouth warm and full of desire, her tongue taunting him when she slipped it into his mouth. He crushed her to him, felt the heat of her body burn against his flesh, felt the warmth surround him as he pressed against her stomach.

"Do you want the lamp out?" she asked.

"No," he husked. "I've waited so long for this moment, I want to watch you."

"You make me blush," she said.

He pushed her back gently and they rolled into bed. He propped himself up on one elbow so he could see the glaze of desire in her eyes. The lamplight flickered across her body as he glanced down and saw the firm, upthrust breasts that begged for his touch. He bent down and kissed each breast, teasing the nipples with his tongue.

"I want you now, Bolt," she husked. "I can't wait any longer."

And their bodies melded together as if they had only one heart between them. Their senses jangled with the excitement as flesh slapped against flesh. Their musks mingled, increased their twin passions until they were consumed by its fire. He glanced down at her face and in the soft lampglow, he saw her eyes glaze with pleasure. He shut his own then as they continued to make love.

"Thank you, Hallie," he whispered finally, still out of breath as they lay still.

"Thank you," she said, her voice still quavering from the excitement. "We shouldn't have waited so long."

"No, but the waiting made it that much sweeter."

"Yes. You are some man, Bolt."

"And you, some woman."

Hallie made him forget about his troubles for most of the night as they made love a second time before dawn. This time their pace was not so frenzied, but the pleasure was even more delicately supreme because they took the time to enjoy each other.

"I wish you didn't have to go," Hallie said from the bed as she watched him dress.

The early light of morning filtered through the curtain and splashed across Hallie's face, danced across her smooth neck, her exposed breasts where the sheet did not quite reach. He saw the new glow of contentment in her eyes and wanted her again. But he knew that he was already leaving later than he'd planned.

"I wish I didn't, either."

"Will you come back sometime?" she asked.

"Of course, I'll be back."

"Soon?"

"Soon," he promised, "and the next time will be

even better."

"It couldn't be better, Bolt, could it?"

"You'll just have to wait and see," he grinned. He left quickly, before he was tempted to crawl back in bed with her and spend the rest of the day making love.

He stopped at the sheriff's office, where he was told that Rankin was having trouble trying to round up enough men for a posse because nobody wanted to face the three brutal, murderous Mexican bandits. Disgusted, Bolt left and stopped at the Drift In Saloon on his way out of town.

At that time of morning the saloon was empty, except for the barkeep. Joe looked up from mopping the floors when Bolt pushed through the batwing doors.

"Have you seen the Mexican bandits?" Bolt asked.

"Not since yestiddy," Joe said. "And I already told you about that. They just seemed to disappear from sight."

"Damn," Bolt said. His heart raced with a sudden fear. Not for himself, but for Lupita and the girls still out at the ranch. He winced at the image that flashed through his mind. Maybe he'd been wrong to spend the night with Hallie. But he couldn't worry about that now. He had to get back out to the ranch as soon as he could.

"You mean you was hopin' to run into 'em here this mornin' 'cause they were here the morning before?" Joe asked as he leaned against his mop.

"Yeah, something like that. I want to see them behind bars where they can't hurt anyone else."

"Cain't blame you there."

"I'll be out at the ranch. If you see them today, please send word out to me."

"I surely will, Bolt."

Bolt pushed his horse as hard as he dared, slowing Nick down before the animal got winded.

When Bolt finally turned onto his path and rode down past the ranch house and into the yard where he could see the bordello, the bunkhouse, and the stable, his heart skipped a beat. It was too quiet. The harlots might still be sleeping this early in the morning if they had worked late the night before, but Tom was usually at the stables about that time, getting ready to ride out and check the cattle. Harmony would be up, too, doing her chores up in the ranch house before the day turned too hot. When she was working up there, she always heard him ride up, always waved to him from the front porch. And where were Chet and Rusty? Usually they were around someplace this time of morning.

The image of horror flashed through his mind again.

He didn't take the time to ride over to the stable to dismount and tie Nick to the post. Instead, he rode directly to the bordello, where he flung himself down from the saddle and scrambled up the steps.

When he opened the door, he heard voices. But still he was scared. As he neared the kitchen, he heard the laughter, recognized the girls' voices. Relief flooded through him, but he took a moment to compose himself before he entered the kitchen. He didn't want the girls to know how worried he was.

"Well, good morning, early birds," he smiled.

All the girls, including Lupita, were there, sitting around the kitchen table, their healthy breakfast almost finished. The other girls seemed relieved to see him, but he noticed that Lupita avoided his gaze.

"Oh, Bolt, we're glad you're back," Harmony said

as she started to get up. "We were all so worried about you."

"Not too worried, I reckon," Bolt grinned. "I heard the laughter before I came in. What are you gals doing up so gol-durned early?"

"We went to bed early last night," Cathy Boring said.

"Oh?" Bolt's face took on a puzzled look.

"No customers last night," Doreen explained.

"We figured nobody wanted to ride out here in the dark with those bandits still on the loose," Harmony said as she got a mug, poured a cup of coffee, and took it to Bolt.

"Thanks. You're probably right." He blew on the steaming brew, took a small sip.

"Did they find the bandits yet?" Harmony asked.

Bolt saw Lupita look up at him, an expectant look in her eyes. She looked tired this morning, puffy around the eyes, as if she hadn't slept well.

"No. Not yet," he said and saw Lupita's shoulders sag as she lowered her head and stared into her lap. Bolt knew how frightened she must be, but he also saw that she was still angry at him.

"You want some breakfast?" Harmony offered as she began to clear a place for him to sit down at the table.

"No. Maybe later. Where's Tom?"

"Still asleep," Harmony said. "He's sleeping on the couch in the living room. Didn't you see him when you came in?"

"No. How could he sleep through this chatter?"

Harmony left for a minute, came right back.

"Yes, he's still there. He figured he'd better sleep down here last night so he could protect us."

"A hell of a lot of good he'd be to you. Sleepin'

143

through this racket."

Lupita dabbed at the corner of her mouth with her napkin, placed it neatly beside her plate. She scooted her chair back and stood up. "Excuse me, please." She walked out of the room without looking at Bolt.

Bolt watched her go, then turned to Harmony. "Damn, those biscuits and gravy smell good. You got enough for me and Tom?"

"Plenty. I'll cook some fresh biscuits if you can wait that long. They're already made. All I have to do is cook them."

"Perfect. I'll wake Tom up and we'll get washed up. Be back in a few minutes."

As Bolt entered the living room, he saw the hem of Lupita's brown dress disappear up the last step. He shook his head.

"Get up, you lazy no-good swine," Bolt called as he shook Tom's shoulder.

"Wh . . . what?" Tom raised his head, blinked his eyes, then saw Bolt. "What's the matter?"

"Fine watchdog you make, you lazy swine. That's what I said," Bolt grinned.

Tom sat up, shook his head, trying to clear the cobwebs from his mind.

"What time is it?" he asked, rubbing the sleep from his eyes.

"Supper's on," Bolt said. "Let's go get washed up."

Tom stood up. "Supper? I don't remember eating breakfast."

The two friends walked out to the bath house, where they had it rigged up so they could take a shower. While they washed their hands and faces in a large bowl, Bolt told him everything about his trip to town. Everything except about what he and Hallie had been doing. That was none of Tom's goddamned business.

"Things are gettin' tricky," he told Tom as they walked back up the steps to the bordello. "I think we'd all better stick pretty close to the bordello today. Chet and Rusty, too. Tell them to find some chores to do around the stable or the yard, but not to go out in the pastures."

"You expectin' trouble?"

"I hope not. Just a precaution. Give us a chance to fix some things around the place."

"I guess we'd all better pack extra iron," Tom said as they went into the living room.

"Reckon so. Tell Harmony I'll be there in a few minutes. I want to talk to Lupita for a minute."

"I wouldn't even try," Tom said.

"Why not?"

"It don't appear that she's too fond of you. Never saw a woman so mad as when you rode off and left her yesterday afternoon."

"Hell, I'm just trying to help her."

"She's some spitfire, that one."

Bolt went on upstairs, promised himself he'd fix that damned step sometime today. He tapped lightly on Lupita's door.

"Who is it?" she called from inside.

"Bolt."

"I have nothing to say to you."

"Dammit, I just want to talk to you about the bandits. Nieves, Diamante, and Maromero."

"I'm listening."

Bolt heard her footsteps pad across the floor and come closer to the door.

"Open up, Lupita. I ain't about to talk through a damned door."

The door creaked open a few inches and Lupita

145

appeared in the crack, but did not look at him.

"What about them?" she asked.

"They're looking for the money."

"I already know that," she said, a sarcastic ring in her words. She looked up and stared defiantly at Bolt.

"Don't get testy with me, Miss O'Rouke. I mean they're looking for you so you can tell them where that damned money's hidden. And since you won't tell me, maybe those bastards can force it out of you."

Lupita threw her door open, stepped back so Bolt could enter. He saw that she was ready to talk to him.

"Did you see them?" she asked.

"No, but they've been in town asking a lot of questions."

"What kind of questions?"

"They were asking for directions to my ranch. They know you're here, Lupita. And they're all together now. All damned three of the swine."

"Do you really think they'll come out here?" she asked, her voice shaky.

Bolt saw the fear in her eyes, knew that the girl was scared out of her wits.

"Oh, they'll come," Bolt assured her. "It's just a matter of time. I just thought you should know so you can decide what you want to do."

"What can I do, Bolt?" she cried, almost in tears.

"Figure it out. You're a big girl now. You don't need my help."

"But I do. Please tell me what I should do."

"I tried to tell you before, remember?"

"Yes," she said softly, as she lowered her head like a scolded child.

"I talked to you until I was blue in the face, Lupita, but you were too goddamned stubborn to listen. Now, you've got to make that decision all by yourself."

"But I can't."

"You have to, Lupita. You know that if those bandits show up out here at the ranch, they'll get that money. They have ways. Don't reckon they'll be any too gentle with you, either."

Bolt saw the girl's face go chalk white, just before he turned to leave the room.

Chapter Thirteen

Lupita reached out and grabbed Bolt's arm, whirled him around with a strength that surprised him.

"Those damned thieves must never get that money!" she shouted, her eyes full of a fierce determination. "It's for my mother!"

"Your mother?" Bolt said. His brow wrinkled with puzzlement. "You mean your father would rob a bank and risk his life just to please your mother?"

"No. My mother needs an operation. She didn't know my father planned to rob a bank."

Bolt studied the expression in her eyes to see if she was lying.

"Is that what your father told you?" He watched her eyes.

"Yes. It's true. We are very poor people. We have no money to our name except the coins you found in my satchel. I swear it on my heart, it's true."

Lupita dropped down on the edge of the bed, lowered her head, and buried her face in her hands. Bolt saw the tears brimming up in her eyes when she looked back up at him.

"Why can't you believe me?" she cried. "I've never lied to you."

"You just haven't told me the truth," he said dryly.

"I couldn't. I promised my father that I would take the money back to my mother in Nuevo Laredo and see that she got the operation. He was sick about it, but my father figured that robbing a bank was the only way to get enough money to pay for my mother's operation. It's very expensive. More than he could've made in a lifetime."

Bolt felt sorry about the girl, to carry such a heavy burden all by herself.

"What's wrong with your mother?" he asked.

"She has something bad growing inside her. A cancer, the doctors tell us. It costs much money to cure her."

"I'm sorry about your mother, Lupita. I really am," Bolt said.

"That's why I have to keep the money away from the thieves and take it back to Nuevo. I just have to make her well again. Oh, she was such a beautiful woman until this sickness came to her two years ago. Alicia. Even her name is pretty, don't you think?"

"Yes, it's a beautiful name," Bolt agreed, not knowing quite what to say.

"I wish you could see her now. She's so frail, so very, very sick."

"Where is she now? Still in Nuevo Laredo?"

"Yes. She is waiting for our return. We have many good friends down there who are caring for her while we are gone. Mother thinks that Papa and I came up to the States to beg a rich bank to lend us the money." Lupita put her hands to her mouth and looked like she was going to cry. "Oh, Mother will be so hurt by Papa's death. I must never tell her how he died. She must never know where the money came from."

149

Bolt strolled across the room, pulled the curtain aside, and idly stared out the window. He glanced back over at her once, saw the sag of her shoulders, the droop of her lip, the tears spilling over the brim of her eyes. Although she still talked a good fight, she was already drained of her determination. Knowing the odds she faced against the vicious bandits, she'd given up hope of reaching Nuevo Laredo with the money.

He walked over and stood in front of her.

"Lupita?"

She looked up at him. "Yes?"

"What if I pay for the operation? Will you give up the stolen money then?"

Her eyes widened in disbelief.

"You would do that?"

"Yes. Take me to her. I'll get her the best doctor in the world."

"Oh, would you?"

"I promise."

Lupita jumped up and threw her arms around Bolt, squeezed him tight, brushed his cheek with her lips before she backed away.

"As a matter of fact," Bolt said, "we have a good doctor in San Antonio. Dr. August Parmenter. The best there is. I'm sure he can help your mother."

"Oh, Bolt, you're wonderful," she beamed. She squeezed him again, then stood back and gazed up at him, her hands clapped together under her chin, as if she were praying. "I can't believe you'd do this for me."

"I'm doing it for your mother."

"I know," she said, some of the merriment gone from her smile.

"Damn, I wish I'd known about this before. It would have saved me a trip to town."

"I'm sorry. Really," Lupita said.

"Yeah. I just left Dr. Parmenter's house a little while ago."

Lupita studied Bolt's face, glanced at his neck, his arms.

"Are you hurt, Bolt?" she asked, the concern showing in her eyes. "Were you wounded?"

"No," he laughed. "I was paying them a social call. I went to visit August and his beautiful daughter, Hallie. Poor thing, her husband died three months ago, and she moved back in with her father."

"You pay a social call at that time of the morning? It must have been dreadfully early."

"I spent the night with them," Bolt smiled.

He saw the flash of jealousy in her eyes. He was sure of it.

"That must have been pleasant for you."

"It was," Bolt smiled and wondered if she suspected how pleasant it had been. "Now, you'd better be packing your bag. We'll leave as soon as we can get Dr. Parmenter to join us."

"Will his daughter be going with us?"

"No. She works."

"Works?" And just what does she do?"

Bolt didn't like the accusing tone in Lupita's voice.

"Runs the Mercantile Store, if it makes any difference."

"It doesn't."

"I'll let you know when we're ready to go."

Tom was already eating breakfast when Bolt got there.

"Thanks for waiting," Bolt said.

"You're welcome," Tom mumbled with a mouthful of biscuits.

"I kept your food warm," Harmony said as she set the food in front of him.

"Thanks, Harmony. Tom, I got a favor to ask of you."

Tom shot him a dirty look. "Oh no, you don't. Doin' you a favor always spells trouble for me. I ain't doin' it no more. Not after the last time."

Bolt knew Tom would say that. He always did when Bolt asked him to do something for him. It was a ritual with them, and the truth was, Tom usually got himself in a mess of trouble.

"I just want you to ride into town and get Dr. Parmenter."

"How come? You sick?" Tom eyed him suspiciously.

"No, Tom. I ain't sick."

"You look it. Didn't get much sleep last night, didya?"

"As a matter of fact, I did," Bolt grinned. "I slept like a baby."

"Yair, you did. So what're you needin' the sawbones for?"

Bolt explained about Lupita's mother and told Tom to have Dr. Parmenter bring his medical bag and anything he might need to be on the trail for four or five days.

"Yair, I'll do it," Tom grumbled. " 'Sides, might just happen to bump into that pretty little daughter of his while I'm there." He gave Bolt a sly look.

"Hallie? Hell, Tom, she wouldn't give the time of day to the likes of you."

"Don't be so sure. You ain't the only one who can lasso a filly."

"Yair, Tom, only you get your animals all mixed up. I saw the last one you snagged. She oinked when she was supposed to whinny."

"At least she's better'n the skinny ones you rope in. She's got somethin' for me to hang on to while I'm

152

puttin' the boots to her."

"Get out of here Tom, or you'll have your trouble before you leave."

Bolt was getting worried by the time he heard the wagon rattle down his path. He'd figured they'd be on their way to Nuevo Laredo by noon. He dug his gold watch out of his pocket, flipped the lid open, and looked at the dial. Almost four in the afternoon.

It surprised him to hear the creak of the wagon wheels. He'd listened for the hoofbeats of two horses all afternoon. He knew Tom would be riding a horse, and thought Dr. August Parmenter would just ride out on the horse he planned to take to Nuevo Laredo.

Lupita O'Rourke was packed and ready to go. Had been for hours. She'd practically worn out her shoes traipsing back and forth from the bordello to the yard, keeping a watch out for Tom and the doctor who would make her mother better. She wore a pair of faded denim trousers and a blue chambray shirt that looked much like the one Bolt was wearing, except that hers was smaller.

Lupita had first put on her plain brown dress, telling Bolt that it wouldn't show the trail dust so much. But he didn't want her to wear any outfit that the Mexican bandits might recognize. She'd argued with him when he told her to dress like a man and to wear a different hat from the one she'd worn before. Bolt borrowed the clothes from Chet, who was not much bigger than Lupita. The clothes fit her better than the ones she'd worn when she'd ridden with the outlaws, and with a little loose binding around her breasts, she'd pass for a young, handsome boy.

Chet and Rusty ambled over to Bolt when they heard the approaching wagon, peering out in that direction.

"I'll be damned," Bolt said when he saw the buggy coming. "He brought his horse and carriage."

"You sure that's Doc?" Rusty asked, squinting his eyes to see that far.

"Yep. That's him," Bolt grinned. "Sure as hell hope he ain't plannin' to take that buggy along. It would really slow us down."

Lupita burst through the door and ran down the steps for the fiftieth time that day. "Are they here?" she called as she ran over and stood beside Bolt, the light-colored Stetson in her hand. She had put the hat on earlier in the day, tucking her long dark hair under its crown. But in the heat of the afternoon, she'd taken it back off.

"They're coming," Bolt said.

Tom rode in ahead of the buggy, went straight for the stable. Bolt and the others ambled over to meet him.

"What took you so long?" Bolt asked as Tom dismounted and stretched his legs. "You have any trouble?"

"Nope. Not this time. But just wait till you see who I brought along."

Bolt didn't like Tom's shit-eating grin. He frowned, turned to stare as the buggy rolled to a gentle stop near the stable.

He saw her then. In the shadows of the interior of the carriage.

"Hallie? What in the hell is she doing here?" Bolt asked Tom.

Lupita stepped closer. "I thought you said she wasn't coming along."

"She isn't," Bolt assured her.

"Sorry we're late," August Parmenter said as he hopped down from the driver's seat. "All my fault."

154

"It's all right," Bolt said as he stepped over to open the carriage door for Hallie. "I'd just hoped to cover some distance before we had to stop for the night."

"Good afternoon, Bolt," Hallie smiled from inside the carriage.

Bolt felt a twinge in his loins when he saw Hallie. She looked as fresh as a buttercup in the bright yellow dress that clung to her figure. Her hair had been swept back away from her face and hung in long, tight, golden curls, held in place with a yellow ribbon.

"Hi," he said as he offered his hand and helped her down. "You look lovely this afternoon."

"Why, thank you, Bolt." Hallie leaned over and gave Bolt a proper kiss on the cheek. "It's good to see you again so soon."

"Hallie, I'd like you to meet Miss O'Rourke." Bolt turned around to Lupita. The mestiza was staring at Hallie, perhaps glaring would be a better word, Bolt thought. He saw the flames of jealousy in Lupita's eyes.

"Oh, I hadn't noticed you," Hallie said to the girl.

Bolt turned when he heard the snobbish tone of Hallie's words. It was unbecoming to her, he thought. He saw that Hallie was eyeing the young mestiza, seemingly sneering at her clothes.

"Lupita, this is Hallie Dumont, Dr. Parmenter's daughter."

"Pleased to meet you, ma'am," Lupita said, a cold edge to her voice. "Bolt's told me all about you."

"Mercy me. I hope he didn't tell you everything." Hallie flashed a phony smile.

"I'm sure he didn't," Lupita said.

Bolt turned and walked away from the girls, walked over to help Tom and the doctor unload the things from the carriage. Tom was grinning at him, and Bolt wanted to punch him in the mouth.

"I'm sorry I threw you late," Parmenter said from the back of the carriage as he handed his heavy saddlebags to Bolt.

"Not to worry," Bolt said.

Parmenter smiled at him. "Had a couple of patients to mend at the last minute."

"How come you brought the carriage, August?"

"Aw, I discovered my horse was sick at the last minute. The one I wanted to ride. So I just loaded my gear on the buggy. I figured you'd have a horse I could ride. I brought my own saddle. Hallie will take the carriage back home. She wanted to come along."

"You can ride Dusty," Tom suggested.

"Yair," Bolt said. "He's the best horse we got, sides mine. Let's get everything ready so we can leave right away. Tom, bring Dusty out and get him ready to go." He started barking orders. "Rusty and Chet, take care of Nick and Lupita's horse. We'll leave in ten minutes."

"They'll be ready," Rusty said.

Bolt turned around. The two girls stood a few feet apart, not paying any attention to each other. He saw Lupita sneak a quick peek at Hallie, angry arrows darting from her eyes, then look away again. He laughed to himself. If they only knew how silly they were being. He had to admit that Lupita had the disadvantage. She looked so unfeminine in those clothes, and Hallie was dressed to the hilt.

"Lupita, better get your hat on now. We're almost ready to leave. Oh, before you go, I want you to meet Dr. Parmenter."

Bolt and the doctor walked over to the girls and Parmenter shook Lupita's hand.

"Pleased to meet you, doctor." Lupita smiled a thin smile. "I hope you can help my mother."

"I'll do everything I can for her," he smiled. "You

156

can be assured of that." The doctor turned to his daughter. "Remember, Hallie, not a word about this to anyone. Lupita's life is in danger. Nobody knows she exists except the bank robbers and the people here at the ranch."

"I know, Father," said Hallie, "and if anyone asks about you, I'm to tell them that you had to go north to take care of sick kin."

"Right."

"Go ahead, Lupita," Bolt said. "See you in a few minutes."

"Anything I can do to help you, Bolt?" Hallie asked, her voice dripping with honey.

"If you wouldn't mind, you could walk over and tell Harmony that we're ready for the food she fixed for us to take along."

"I'd be happy to," she replied.

Lupita glared at Hallie for an instant, then turned and started for the bordello.

Hallie waited until Lupita was clear inside before she headed the same way.

When they were alone, Bolt turned to August. "You know, I really don't like the idea of Hallie riding back to town by herself, under the circumstances."

"It's still light out," Parmenter said. "I don't think she minds."

"But, I do. With those damned bandits roaming around out there someplace, I'd feel better if Tom escorted her home. Would you mind?"

"No. Not at all. If Tom doesn't mind. I would feel better about it, too."

"Tom won't mind. I really appreciate your riding down to Nuevo Laredo to take a look at Lupita's mother. The poor girl is desperate."

"Glad to help, if I can. Tom told me that Lupita's mother has the cancer. Is that right?"

157

"That's what Lupita said."

"Seems you were right about the girl, Bolt. I saw the sadness in her eyes."

Bolt told the doctor all he knew about the mestiza. He was explaining their mission when Tom returned from the corral with the horse named Dusty.

"Tom, I got a favor to ask of you," Bolt said.

Tom tied the horse to the post before he turned around. He glared at Bolt for a long, hard minute before he spoke.

"Oh no, you don't." He shook his head. "Doin' you a favor is like askin' somebody to break your leg. A favor for you is always trouble for me. I ain't doin' it no more. Not after the last time."

"You didn't have any trouble last time."

"Not if you don't count losing ten greenbacks in a poker game while I was waitin' for Doc to mend a leg," Tom grumbled.

"Hell, you can't go blamin' that on the favor asked," Bolt chided his friend.

"If he'd rather not do it, that's all right," Dr. Parmenter said.

"Tom'll do it, or I'll break bone."

"So, what's the favor I gotta do?" Tom asked.

"Something you'll really enjoy this time, I reckon," Bolt said. "I want you to escort Hallie back to town. Simple enough?"

Tom's eyes brightened. "It'd be my pleasure."

Bolt continued to tell the doctor of his plans, his concerns for their safety.

Lupita and Hallie came out of the house just then. They kept a wide, cold, silent distance between them as they walked across the yard.

"The Mexicans know the country better than we do," Bolt told the doctor, "so it could be dangerous out there."

158

All three men turned to watch the two girls walk toward them.

"You talking about what's dangerous?" Tom laughed.

"What do you mean?" Bolt asked.

"You ask me," he said, "I'd say it'd be more dangerous to stay here and watch them two fillies fight it out over Bolt."

Chapter Fourteen

Tom's muscles tensed. He felt the hackles rise on the back of his neck, as if a chill breeze had blown across his flesh.

He didn't like what he saw. He didn't tell Hallie about it because he didn't want to alarm her if it wasn't really them.

"The breeze feels good after the hot afternoon," he said to Hallie instead. It was almost dusk. He and Hallie had stayed to eat supper with the girls so that Hallie and Harmony could talk. Still light out, so they should be safe. They were halfway to town and he had begun to relax when he'd first spotted them.

"Yes, it does," she said. "I appreciate you escorting me home. I'm glad for the company."

Tom had tied his horse to a lead rope on the back of the carriage so he could sit up in the driver's seat with Hallie. He held the reins slack in his hands so the lead horse could have its head.

"I'm glad to do it," Tom said.

He squinted his eyes, couldn't be sure.

"It was silly of Father to ask you to take me home," she laughed as she turned to look at him. "He forgets I'm a big girl now."

"I think it was Bolt's idea."

Since he'd first spotted it five minutes ago, the spool of dust from the riders had grown from a speck to a size big enough for Tom to distinguish the shapes, count the riders. Yes, there were three of them. Too early to see the color of their horses, but they were coming on fast.

"Well, it doesn't matter whose idea it was. Those bandits are tracking Lupita, not me. They're more likely to show up at the ranch than anyplace else." She talked to the side of his face because he wouldn't look at her.

"More likely," he said, not really hearing her. They were roans, all right, and the riders, Mexicans. They were close enough to tell. Tom switched the reins to his other hand, fingered the butt of his pistol to be sure it was there.

"Besides," Hallie said, "those bandits wouldn't be riding out on this road when it's still light out. It's too well traveled."

Oh yes they would, he wanted to tell her.

She turned to see what Tom was staring at.

"Tom, do you see those three riders out there? It looks like they're coming this way," she said. She leaned forward, squinted her eyes.

"Yair, I see 'em."

They loomed bigger and bigger, closer and closer. The riders were almost there. Tom eased his pistol out of the holster, let it rest on his lap.

"Tom. Do you think they're the bandits?" Hallie asked, a sudden alarm in her voice.

"No way of telling, but I can't go pluggin' 'em off. I wouldn't want to kill an innocent man."

"Just act normal, Tom," she said as she leaned back into the leather seat. "Even if they're the bandits, they might just ride on by."

Tom held his breath as the riders barreled down on

161

them, hoping they'd go on by.

Suddenly, the carriage was in the middle of a cloud of dust, surrounded by horsemen on three sides as the riders skidded their horses to a halt. Tom jerked back on the reins. The buggy lurched to a stop, throwing Tom and Hallie forward with a jerk, then backward into the seat as the carriage settled on its hinges.

Tom looked to his right, his left, and straight ahead. And each time, he stared directly into the round, dark barrel of a pistol.

"Howdy," Tom said. "Nice day for a ride."

"Yes. He is one of them," said the nearest rider, his accent thick, his face cruel and pinched.

Tom saw the round stain of blood on the man's shirt, just below the shoulder. He noticed the thick bulge of bandages and knew the rider was the escaping bandit whom Bolt had wounded.

"Where is Lupita?" demanded the one directly in front of the carriage, his pistol trained between Tom's eyes. He was the tallest of the three Mexicans. His face was laced with scars, his nose crooked, as if it'd been broken.

Hallie pushed back against the seat, hunched down into it.

"I don't know what you're jawin' about," Tom said.

"You know," said the one to his left.

"Where is money?" the third man demanded.

"I don't know," Tom said. "I don't know anything about any money."

"The man, he does not want to talk," said the first attacker.

"Maybe we give him reason to talk," said the one on the right.

"Yes, you tell us or we shoot you dead."

"I can't tell you something I don't know," Tom protested.

162

"You will talk," said the one straight ahead of him. "Throw down your pistol."

Tom clutched it in his hand, but couldn't fire it. Not with three pistols aimed and ready to blow his head to the wind.

"Do what they say, Tom," Hallie whispered.

The rider on Hallie's side rode closer, trained his weapon at her head.

"We kill your lady friend if you do not do as we say. We have no use for her."

Tom eased his pistol up in the air, looked for the chance to use it, but knew he didn't stand a chance. He tossed it over the side, heard it clatter to the ground. Diamante kicked it under the carriage.

"Get down," said the ugly, bronze-skinned man in front of them.

Hallie started to scoot to the edge of her seat. Tom held her back.

"We shoot if you do not get down," threatened the one in front. "Now."

Tom stuck his hands in the air, moved slowly to the side when he saw the men take aim.

"Easy," called one of the bandits.

"Around here," ordered another as Tom slid down to the ground.

Hallie climbed down the other side.

The gunmen herded them around to the front. The one who was called Juan stood guard as the other two Mexicans slid down from their horses.

Fidel Diamante, the tall one, strolled over, stood in front of them.

"Do not play the games with us," he said. "You tell us where Lupita is gone. She is not at the rancho. We looked there already."

Tom thought the Mexican was bluffing. The bandits had come from the opposite direction. He and

163

Hallie had been at the ranch until twenty minutes ago and they had seen nobody around.

"I don't know this Lupita you speak of," Tom lied.

Fidel Diamante suddenly raised his hand and slammed the butt of his pistol against the side of Tom's head.

"Stop!" Hallie cried. "Don't hurt him."

Tom's hands flew to his head. He reeled back, staggered, started to fall. He managed to stay on his feet, got his balance. His head throbbed with the pain.

"Now you talk," ordered Diamante. "Where is Lupita? Where is the money?"

"I don't know," Tom said, barely able to stand the pain in his head.

With the other two Mexicans training their guns on Tom and Hallie, Diamante stuffed his pistol into the holster. He stepped closer, slid a knife from the scabbard in his waistband. Held it up for Tom to see. He ran his fingers slowly along the flat sides of the blade.

"Maybe we cut your tongue out if you do not want to talk," he said, a curl of a snarl on his lips.

Tom's heart pounded his chest, matching the throbbing of his head. He didn't utter a word.

"No!" Hallie screamed. "Don't do it!"

"We will see if the blade is sharp," Diamante said. He glared at Tom, grabbed his arm.

Tom tried to wrest his arm away from the bandits.

Diamante jabbed the point of the blade at Tom's hand to make his point.

"No! No! Leave him alone!" Hallie tried to get to Tom. Nieves shoved a cold pistol against her head. She didn't move a muscle after that.

With the knife so close to his flesh, Tom held his hand perfectly still. The knife touched his wrist,

164

flicked the flesh, drew blood.

"Nooooo," Hallie wailed.

Tom winced. The pain was deep and quick, before the spot turned numb. His mind screamed with the pain in his head.

"He will not talk. Make him sorry for it," Diamante told his companions before he slid his knife into its sheath. He smiled cruely at Hallie.

Nieves and Maromero grabbed Tom's arms, jerked him away from the carriage. Nieves plowed a fist into Tom's chin. Tom staggered under the blow, fell backwards. They pulled him back for more.

The two bandits' fists plowed into Tom's flesh, rock-hard thrusts to his gut, his eye, his back, anyplace they could find to strike.

Tom reeled under the vicious attack. With each new blow, he couldn't tell where the pain was coming from anymore. Hard knuckles crashed into his temple, sent him sprawling to the ground. The back of his head slammed into the hard earth. The loud crack of the blow rattled through his ear, scrambled his brains. He tried to get up, rolled onto his back. A fog clouded his mind. He thought he heard Hallie's scream.

"No! Hallie screamed. "Let him go. I will tell you what you want to know. Please," she begged.

A boot crashed into Tom's skull. Rockets of color exploded in his head.

"Stop," Diamante ordered. "The girl will talk now. Let us hear what she has to say."

The blows stopped, mercifully. Tom couldn't think, couldn't hear, couldn't smell the dry earth. Deep in his mind, he knew he had to stop Hallie from talking. The words wouldn't form. Neither would his mind.

"Speak, girl," Diamante ordered. "Speak the truth or you will be like your friend. Where is Lupita?"

"She is on her way home," Hallie cried.

165

"Nuevo Laredo?" Diamante asked.

"Yes."

Hallie's knees shook so badly, she thought they would give out on her. She knew she shouldn't divulge the secrets, but she couldn't let them keep attacking Tom. His body couldn't take any more of the vicious blows.

"Did she carry the money with her?"

"I don't know," she said honestly. Nobody had mentioned the money.

Diamante raised his fist, held it as a threat.

"Look at your friend. You will look like him if you do not tell us where the money is."

"I don't know. I'm telling you the truth. I don't know if Lupita dug it up and took it with her, or whether it is still buried."

"Lupita carries the money with her," Pedro Nieves said. "I know it is so. She needed it for her mother. She would not leave the money here."

"Maybe you are right, Pedro," Diamante said after he pondered the remark. "Lupita will need the money in Nuevo Laredo. It would do her little good here. She would not go home unless she carried it with her."

"I think so," said Pedro.

"Who went with her?" Diamante asked Hallie. He stared at her, ran his fingers over the handle of his sheathed knife.

Hallie's eyes widened when she saw the knife start to slide out of the sheath.

"Bolt and my father," she blurted out. She heard Tom groan, glanced over at him. He didn't move.

"Yes, we know the man they call Bolt," said Pedro Nieves. "I saw him kill my friend. We will kill Bolt when we find him. Just for the fun of it."

Hallie shuddered.

The sky took on the first tinges of gray dusk as the

color faded from the land. It would be dark soon.

"Did Lupita pay these men to give her protection on her journey?" Diamante asked.

"No. She didn't pay them anything. They wanted to help her. That is all."

"How long have they been gone?" Diamante asked as he tapped the knife back into its sheath.

"An hour, maybe two," Hallie said.

"It will not take us long to catch up to them," Diamante said. "But we must hurry."

"Shall we kill them?" Pedro Nieves asked, a look of demented glee in his eyes.

"No, let them go," said Diamante. "They can do us no harm." He strolled over to Tom, kicked him savagely in the ribs to prove his point.

"No, no!" cried Hallie. "No more. I've told you all I know."

Diamante spit on Tom, glared at Hallie.

"If you do not tell the truth, we will find you," he said, touching his hand to his knife.

"I have told you all I know," Hallie said, wishing they'd leave.

Diamante mounted his horse, motioned for the others to follow him.

A flood of relief washed across Hallie's body when they were gone, making her weak in the knees. Her body began to tremble in the aftermath of the violence.

For a full minute she stood dazed, watching the road where she'd seen the bandits disappear, where the sound of the hoofbeats had faded away. It was so still now, it all seemed like a bad dream.

Tom moaned. The sound startled her, brought her out of her haze. She dashed over to him, bent down.

"Tom! Tom, are you all right?" she called. She ran her fingers lightly over a swollen lump on his forehead. She felt him wince. She wondered how bad the wounds were, whether any of the blows had torn his insides apart.

"Tom! Tom!"

Darkness was coming with the charcoal of the sky.

"Tom, it's getting dark. We've got to get you home," she called.

Tom's eyes fluttered open, but they couldn't focus on anything. He looked up at Hallie, his mind spinning. She was no more than a blur.

His eyes drifted closed. His head fell to the side, his chin rested on his shoulder. He lay perfectly still.

"Tom! Tom!"

The sound echoed through the darkening night.

Chapter Fifteen

Hallie ran her finger lightly over Tom's neck, found the spot where his pulse would be. She pressed gently, felt the throbbing.

Tom was still alive.

"Tom, Tom, please wake up," she said.

He didn't move.

She stood up and looked around. The darkness was closing in on her and she was frightened. She walked over to the carriage and looked inside, wondered if she were strong enough to lift him onto the seat, wondered if she were strong enough to drag his body over to the buggy. She tilted her head, listened for hoofbeats, hoping that someone would come along to help her.

She went back over to Tom and dropped to her knees. She leaned over his body and wanted to cry.

"Tom," she whispered in his ear. "Please help me."

Tom's head moved to get away from the tickle of her hot breath in his ear.

"Tom. Are you awake?"

"Ahhhhnnnnnnnnnn," he groaned.

Hallie's heart soared.

"Tom? Are you awake?"

"Huhhhh? Wha . . . what?" His eyes fluttered open and he stared up at her shadowy face, not knowing where he was. He started to sit up, was driven back down by the throbbing pain in his head.

"Easy," Hallie said. "Take it easy."

Tom looked up at her again, studied her face.

"Who are you?" he asked.

"Hallie. It's me. Hallie."

"Hallie? I don't know you, do I?"

"Oh, no, Tom. It was the blow to your head."

"Tom who? Who are you?"

"I'm a friend of Bolt's," she said, hoping the familiar name would bring Tom out of his daze.

"Bolt who?" Tom said. "Hallie. That's a pretty name.

"You'll be all right if we can just get you home where I can take care of you," she sighed.

"Take care of me now," he said.

Hallie heard the thick husk in his voice, knew it was caused by the brutal blows to his head.

"You're going to be fine, Tom."

"I want you now, Hallie."

"Tom, you're out of your mind."

"That's what they all tell me." The swollen lip twisted his smile.

Tom felt the warmth flood through his loins. Felt his cock stiffen and begin to swell. He fought his way up through the webs of gauze that clouded his mind. A warm hand brushed against his hardening mass, sent chill bumps across his naked body. There was dampness there, too, which only added to his arousal.

He couldn't remember where he was, but felt the softness of the bed beneath him. He didn't want to open his eyes and spoil the moment. He smelled the perfume. That told him what he wanted to know.

Had he been out drinking the night before? Had

170

too much? He didn't know. He couldn't remember. Felt like it, the way his head throbbed with a sickening pain.

He didn't care right then. The pleasure was too great. The warm, flooding sensation spread across his body and he felt the gentle massaging at his inner thighs where he was so sensitive. He felt the hand caress him, squeeze, and then go on to other places. Across his bare belly, up to his chest.

He couldn't remember who he'd been with when he went to bed. He opened his eyes to tiny slits, peeked out, just as the hand slid down to his crotch and brushed against his thick shaft. He saw the beautiful face of Hallie Dumont. Was he dreaming? Hallie would do this to him? It surprised him, but he didn't object. He snapped his eyes shut so that she wouldn't know he was awake yet.

Gawd, he felt awful.

He peeked out again and saw the towel in her hand. He closed them and felt the rubbing pressure again. First one hip, then the other. Between his legs.

He opened his eyes and stared up at her face.

"I want you, Hallie," he said, a thick husk to his voice.

Hallie glanced over at him.

"Oh, Tom, you're awake. I'm so glad."

"So am I, Hallie. I want you very much."

"You're still out of your head."

"No. Look what you've done to me." Tom raised his head to look down at himself. The pain was too much. His head fell back to the pillow.

"Is the pain bad?" she asked as she draped a sheet over his lower body.

"Gawd, yes. What happened? Did we have fun at the party?"

"What party, Tom?" Hallie smiled.

"I don't know. I don't remember. But I must have had a snootful.

Hallie pulled a chair up to the bed and sat down. She explained what had happened the night before.

"Jeeez," he said. He put his hands on his face, dabbed gently across the surface, felt the swollen flesh. "I don't remember it. I remember seeein' the riders, but everything else is gone after that."

"You've had a great shock to your body, Tom. You need some rest to heal." She added a blanket, and pulled both covers up to his neck, brushed out the wrinkles. "You just close your eyes and go back to sleep."

"I still want you, Hallie. I want you to do things to me."

"You have a naughty tongue, Tom," she scolded. "I'm going to be your nurse for a day or two, and I'll hear no more of that talk. I'll be back in a little while to take care of you."

"I'll be waiting."

"Can I go with you Bolt?" Lupita asked.

"I'm just going down to the river to fill the canteens. You can come along if you want to."

It was way after dark now and they had only the light of the moon to light their path. They hadn't dared to build a fire to cook with, or even to have a pot of coffee, which Bolt liked after his supper.

This was their third night on the trail and Bolt figured they could make Nuevo Laredo late the next day. If they didn't make it in time to cross the Mexican border, at least they'd be near Laredo. The three of them had pushed it pretty hard, stopping only to stretch their legs, rest their horses, chew on jerky and hardtack. Each night they had stopped for several

172

hours and spread their blankets on the hard ground.

"Do you think they'll find us?" Lupita asked. She sat on her blanket, on a flat stretch of land, near the edge of the water. Her knees were drawn up to her chest and she rested her chin on them as she watched Bolt dip the canteens in the water to fill them.

"I hope not, Lupita."

But Bolt had his doubts. He'd seen the spools of dust on the backtrail. Just twice, but it was enough to keep him on edge.

"Could I change to one of my dresses in the morning?" she asked.

"No, Lupita," he snapped. "Not until you're safely home." She had asked the same question twice a day since they'd left the ranch.

"But I look like a little boy in them."

"That's all you need to look like right now."

"I would like to look nice for you."

"You're just fine." Bolt drank from one of the canteens, offered it to Lupita, then filled it again.

"Are you sleepy tonight?" she asked as he filled the last canteen and set it on the bank.

"Tired, but not sleepy."

"Come sit with me a while. You need to relax."

"I think I do." When he sat down, the exhaustion settled into his bones and he stretched out, lay on his back, stared up at the sky.

"Pretty night, isn't it?" Lupita asked as she lay down beside him.

"Yair, I reckon."

"Think it will rain tomorrow? We need it."

"Dunno. 'Spose it could rain. There are enough clouds."

For a long while, neither of them spoke.

"Bolt, what's wrong with me?" she asked.

"Nothing, I reckon."

173

"Then, why won't you make love to me?"

"The doctor's with us. It wouldn't be right."

"He's far enough away. Besides, he snores."

"Lupita, please. We just can't."

"You just won't, you mean," she hissed. "You are very stubborn, Bolt."

"Maybe so."

There was another long stretch of silence.

"You make love to many other girls," she said. "Why not me?"

"We can't."

"You make love to Harmony and Hallie," she charged. "I know you do."

"You don't know anything."

"I heard you with Harmony that night," she said. Bolt glanced over at her and glared.

"You heard nothing."

"Don't tell me what I heard," she snapped. "That was the night I wanted to sneak away. I tiptoed down to the room where you were sleeping. I listened at the door to be sure you were asleep. The noises I heard were not snoring."

"It is not polite to listen at someone's bedroom door, Lupita."

"I know about Hallie, too. You slept in her bed the night you went to town."

"I suppose you heard me not snoring that night, too, from miles away," he said sarcastically.

"No. I saw the look in Hallie's eyes the next day," Lupita said. "I saw the way you looked at her, too. A woman notices such things."

"So? A look means nothing."

"It does when the look is special," Lupita argued. "I have seen you look at me that way before, too. More than once. But you do not take me to your bed. Why? What is wrong with me?"

174

"Maybe you push too damned hard, Lupita. Maybe it just has to happen when it happens."

"And maybe you and I should stick to talking about the weather," she raged. "It'd be safer."

"I reckon so."

Bolt felt uncomfortable with her so close beside him. He felt the tug at his loins and wished it away. There were just too many things that stood between them. Mostly, he guessed, it was the robbery money. She'd promised to give it up if he brought Dr. Parmenter down to take care of her mother. The money was still hidden and she refused to tell him where it was. It was something they didn't talk about anymore.

"Are your legs sore from riding?" Lupita asked a little later. "Mine are."

"Yair. That and my butt. Too many hours in the damned saddle." He closed his eyes and let the night noises surround him. The constant gurgling of the water spilling over boulders put him in a hypnotic trance and it seemed his muscles melted and floated away with the water.

He was almost asleep when he felt the pressure on his thighs. He looked up and saw Lupita sitting next to him, her arms stretched out, her hands grasping the tops of his upper thighs. She kneaded the muscles beneath his trousers, squeezing, sliding, squeezing, as her hands worked their way down to his knees. She worked her way back up, as if she had two loaves of bread to do at the same time.

"You don't mind, do you?" she whispered.

"No," he sighed. "Feels damned good."

"Let me move so I can reach them better," she said. She pushed his legs apart, rolled over and sat on her knees between them.

She used both hands on one leg, now, massaging

175

one at a time. She started at the knee, worked her way up. Pushing, squeezing, pressing.

"You'll put me to sleep," he said, relaxed, contented.

"I don't want to do that," she teased.

She slowly kneaded his leg all the way up to the Y of his crotch, delicate at times, pressure at the right places. When she reached his crotch, heat flared across the triangle of his sex, spread up his belly, flooded his inner thighs. She lingered there, spread her fingers out wider, slid her hands between his legs. His loins burned hot with her touch when she pressed them against the sensitive crease.

She stroked the deep creases of his inner thighs with both hands. Bolt felt the backs of her hands brush against his swollen shaft. She did it again, applied pressure as she brought her hands up.

Bolt found it hard to breathe, so much was he trying to put it out of his mind. So hard he was trying to control his emotions.

"Feel good?" she cooed.

"Yes, but you'd better stop." He heard the husk in his own voice, hoped she hadn't noticed.

"Do I make you hot?"

"Yes, but we can't do it, Lupita. You know that."

"I am only rubbing your sore muscles," she smiled. "There is nothing wrong with that, is there?"

"No."

"Maybe you think I'm getting too bold. Maybe I should only rub the muscles in your back. Roll over on your side, Bolt. I will work the stiffness out of those muscles, too. Then you will feel safer."

Damn her, Bolt thought. He didn't want her to stop what she was doing.

"Yes, you're right." His voice cracked with his urgency, his desire. He unbuckled his gunbelt, reached up, and placed it on a corner of the blanket. He unbuttoned his fly to take the pressure off. Maybe that would help cool him down. As he did these things, he thought he heard the rustle of cloth, other than his own, but he couldn't be sure. He rolled over on his side, his back to the pretty mestiza.

Her hands found the weary muscles around his shoulder blades, and that felt good, too. She tugged the back of his shirt free, slid her hands underneath. She placed her hands on his lower back, the palms of her hands resting in the curve of his waistline. She worked the palms up his back, exerting just the right pressure with each upward movement. She did that twice, she slid her hands to the middle of his back, walked up the spine like an inchworm. Her hands carried much power and yet were warm against his skin as she kneaded his flesh.

"I will do the fronts of your shoulders and the calves of your legs. That is where I ache from keeping my feet in the stirrups all day. And then I will be done, with nothing left to massage. When I am through, Bolt, you will sleep like a baby."

Chapter Sixteen

With his back to her, Bolt could not see Lupita as she worked the flesh of his back muscles. He did not need eyes to feel the delicate pressure of her touch, nor did he need them to smell the heady scent of her musk. He did not need eyes to hear the soothing, bubbling brook.

The calves of his legs were next, so she had said. He, too, ached there, where the muscles were thick and did most of the work.

"Bolt, slip out of your trousers so I can massage the calves of your legs."

"Why?" The thought of it fanned new flames of desire in his loins.

"It is the only way I can get the right pressure to work the thick muscles that are there. If you choose to leave your trousers on, the fabric will only slide around with my hand."

"Oh." Made sense. And it gave him an excuse to free himself of the fabric that bound him.

"If you are shy, I will cover my eyes."

"Not that shy," Bolt laughed. He tugged at them, lifted his hips, and pushed them on down. Lupita helped snag them over his boots.

She went right to work, kneading deep into the taut muscles with her expert manipulations. He felt only the touch of her warm hands, but it was enough. She worked these muscles longer than the others, kneading him from his ankle to the bend in his knee. She gave them a final squeeze and drew her hands away.

"Just your front shoulder muscles to go and then you're ready for bed," she said. And he listened for any seductive tones in her voice. There were none.

"It feels good, Lupita," he said, and knew she heard the husk in his voice. "If I hired you to do this to our customers, we could make a small fortune. You are really an expert."

"Would I have to do other things to them, too?" she teased.

"No. I have other girls who do that."

"Roll over on your back. Let's get it done so you can get some sleep tonight. If you are shy, close your eyes and I will do the same."

"I'm not naked," he laughed. "I'm still wearing my shorts."

"I know."

When he rolled over on his back, he saw that his stiff stalk made a tent out of his shorts, and he wished he'd followed her advice.

She moved over on top of him, straddled his legs, leaned forward, and quickly put the palms of her hands on his shoulders.

His body exploded with a million electrical shocks as her hot, naked flesh touched his. Legs against legs, tummy against tummy, full breasts against his chest, her inner thighs settling over his tent stalk, her damp heat searing through the thin fabric of his shorts. And every one of his relaxed muscles jumping back to life.

Oh, God, how he wanted her.

He thrust up with his rigid staff, squirmed around until he felt the damp heat of her slit through the barrier of his shorts. He thrust again and felt the lips part under his gentle pressure.

She worked his shoulder muscles with soft, powerful hands, rocked her body back and forth on top of his as she stroked his flesh with her hands. The rocking motion, the rhythm of her strokes. The pressure of her rubbing up and down the length of him as she moved. All of it driving him into a wild frenzy. And only the white-flag barrier between them.

Surrender! Surrender!

It went so fast. A full two minutes of massaging his shoulder muscles. But it went so fast.

With her powerful hands, she pushed herself back off away from his chest, sat on what would have been his lap if he had been sitting, the lips of her sex still interwined with his probing stalk. And only the white-flag barrier between them.

Surrender!

Surrender!

"I am done, Bolt," she said. "Unless you have any other muscle that needs massaging."

"You know damned well I do," he husked.

She didn't move, and neither did he, except when he thrust his hips up so he could tug and push his shorts down over his hips, down to his knees where he jiggled his legs to shake them down to his ankles and kick them out of the way.

And no more white-flag barrier between them.

Surrender.

After a minute, Lupita leaned down and with her small, firm breasts crushing into his chest, she placed her lips on his. Her lips were full, and warm, and soft on his mouth. Her tongue slipped inside his damp, parted lips, and when she flicked it back and forth across his own, Bolt wanted to stroke in and out of her.

She backed away, finally, her lips still so close they were almost touching.

"Bolt, will you make love to me?" Her throat was full of a velvet fog.

And there was no more barrier between them.

Surrender.

"I want you, Hallie," Tom said again, on the second night that he stayed at her house.

He was still sore as hell from the vicious beating he'd taken from the three Mexican outlaws. His eye was still swollen almost shut, but he could finally see out of it. The cut at the corner of his eye had scabbed over. The bruise under his eye had turned purple-black. The other eye wasn't swollen very much, but the purple bruise around it was wider, deeper.

He ached all over and still hadn't sorted out all of his bruises. Goose eggs and lump, cuts and bumps, all over his head and shoulders. Hallie had bound his midsection with strips of gauze to protect the cracked ribs.

"No, Tom," she said, applying salve on the huge black-and-blue bruise at his groin.

"It ain't fair, Hallie. Look what you done to me."

"I didn't do it, Tom," she smiled. "It was your naughty thoughts."

"Well, you had a hand in it, too, so to speak. Every damn time you bathe me or change my bandages, I get hot. Least you could let me do it just once. Just for all the times I been hot and you said no."

"No, Tom," she laughed. "It doesn't work that

way."

"With me, it does. Every damned time you touch me it feels so good I want to croak like a frog."

"You sound like one, too," she laughed, "Every time you're that way."

"Hell, I'm that way all the time around you, Hallie. Every time you touch me or squeeze me, I get a great big stiff one."

"Watch your mouth, Tom," she said. "I don't squeeze you there."

"Yes, you do. I felt it this mornin'."

"Tom, you do have your fantasies, don't you?" she said as she salved the rest of the bruise to his groin. He winced and she didn't know whether it was from pain or pleasure.

"No harm in that, is there?"

"No, none at all."

"Well, I'm damned glad you learned all that doctorin' stuff from your father. It wouldn't feel good at all if he were touchin' me like you do. Hell, I wouldn't even get a stiff one."

"That's what I mean, Tom, It's your naughty thoughts that make you this way." Hallie took her hand away, set the salve on the nightstand next to the bed. She drew the sheet up over his naked, bandaged body.

"That's another thing, Hallie. You make me lie around all day without any clothes on. What do you expect me to do?"

"I expect you to get some rest. You'll be well enough to go back home tomorrow."

"Good. I gotta go warn Bolt about them bandits that are trackin' him."

"You can't ride all the way to Nuevo Laredo, Tom. Not for a couple of weeks yet."

"I'd be too late by then. He'd be dead and buried."

"You're too late, anyway, I'm sure."

"Well, I'm gonna try, dammit."

"You can't ride a horse that far. Not with all those bruises."

"Then you can take me down in your buggy. I don't care how I get there. I just gotta warn Bolt."

"You're a stubborn one, you are."

"Dammit, Hallie, I want you. Look at that thing. It's still stiff as a flagpole. I feel like I'm in a goddamn army tent the way it's stickin' up."

"No, Tom," she smiled.

"Why not?"

"It wouldn't be right between us."

"Why not? You're a woman. I'm a man. We fit together."

"No, Tom."

"Hell, all I want is a few minutes of pleasure," Tom said. "I ain't asking for your hand in marriage or no longtime commitment between us, Hallie."

"Maybe that's your trouble."

"You mean you don't want to sleep with me because we ain't married?"

"No, that's not it, Tom."

"Then, what?"

"Tom, you might as well give up," Hallie smiled.

"You're the stubborn one, Hallie. You ain't said yes to me once since I been askin'."

"You know, Tom, you would get further with a woman if you didn't act like you wanted only to jump in bed with them."

"But that's what I want, Hallie."

"First you must know how to play the game."

"Like Bolt? How does he do it anyway? You say yes to him."

"He does not think of himself. He makes a woman feel comfortable with him."

"Hell, he ain't no different than me. We both want the same thing."

"Oh, he's very different," she said softly. "And he gets what he wants."

"Shit."

"You have a naughty tongue, too, Tom Penrod."

Chapter Seventeen

The three men rode through the night. They rode without sleep, with an anger inside them that cast their dark, swarthy faces in bronze. When they reached the outskirts of Laredo, their leader pulled up at an adobe building near the main trail. His lathered horse snorted, tossed its head and mane.

"This is a place I know," said Fidel Diamante. "We get some sleep, and when the sun goes down we will be ready."

"This Bolt, he will not be here before then?" asked Pedro Nieves.

"You heard what the girl told us. He will come, but we have outridden him by a day."

"I think you are right, Fidel," said a weary Juan Maromero. "We will sleep and we will kill this gringo pig."

A dark woman came to the door, looked up at Diamante. Her eyes flickered slightly, but her face did not change expression. She stepped outside, leaving the door open.

"See that our horses are fed and rubbed hard," Fidel told her. "Do not come back until after siesta. You cook for us then, and bring a bottle of the good whiskey and some wine."

The woman said nothing. The three men entered the adobe, and Nieves, the last to enter, kicked the door shut. The woman hobbled away, returned in a few minutes with two young boys. The three of them led the horses away as the sun rose over the horizon and threw long shadows in the shade of the few humble adobes that peppered the edge of a town not yet fully awake.

The men slugged down the last of a bottle of mescal, dropped their gunbelts, and fell onto floor mats. Flies buzzed in the coolness of the two small rooms, and flew in and out of screenless windows. The men grunted, fell into deep sleep. Soon, the silence rattled with the rasp of snoring, and the day wore on until the sun baked the land and sent shimmers of heat that looked like thin waterfalls upward, so that the earth seemed to shake in the somnolence of the afternoon.

The old woman returned when the sun was starting to fall through its last quadrant of sky. The Waterbury clock in the Drover's Saloon stood at three-thirty, and the Mexicans woke from their siestas and brushed flies off their faces as the shade deserted their sandaled feet.

The men in the adobe were still asleep, and they slept until the cast iron barrel stove crackled with heat and the air filled with the aroma of beans.

Juan Maromero arose from the pallet, his eyes still bleary from sleep, the flesh around them puffed like an adder's throat.

The old woman looked at the men as she shoved the frijoles around in the clay pot with a wooden spoon.

"Who are you, what are you called?" asked Maromero. "Are you a cousin of Fidel's?"

The old woman wiped a bony veined hand across

186

her mouth and cracked a mirthless, toothless grin.

"You ask too many question," she said, and behind her words there was a cackle like the grate of a rusted windmill on dry, flat Kansas prairie. "Soon, you eat, and then you will all be killed."

The other two men stirred, half rose from their woven mat beds. Fidel fixed the crone with a hard stare. Pedro Nieves blinked like a ruffled owl and rubbed the dust of sleep from his hollow dark eyes.

"Close the mouth, *viejita*," said Fidel. "Your tongue should have been cut out long ago."

"It is a miracle you did not do that, too," snapped the old woman, whose long hair was slick and greasy with oil and tawny with the dust of Laredo. She chewed on a tough, fibrous chunk of spine-stripped nopal.

"*Callate!*" barked Diamante.

"What is this?" asked Nieves. He scratched his left armpit, stifled a yawn. "Is this woman a witch?"

There was a silence then, and the men rose from the floor and looked at the woman and at Fidel. Fidel said nothing. He stooped down and picked up his gunbelt, strapped it on.

"This man," said the woman, "killed my husband, raped my daughter, and beat me senseless. He took much food and a few small pesos and he laughed. He said he come back to this place and pay me big money for what he did."

"I am back," said Diamante, the trace of a cruel smile on his lips.

"And will you pay me money?" she asked sarcastically.

"I will pay you the dewdrops on my balls," said Fidel.

Later, the men ate the flattened little cakes of corn,

ground to powder on stone, and tough rabbit meat drowned in a strong and fiery sauce of tomatoes and chilis, and red beans that made their bellies swell and air-gas make noise from their behinds. They patted their bellies and made a game of throwing the old woman around between them as they laughed, and from the corner of their eyes, they watched the sun go down.

Finally, Fidel said: "It is time to go and wait for Lupita and her two gringo friends."

The old woman looked at them as she scraped excess grease from the stovetop. Her eyes turned dull and lifeless in the dimming light.

Fidel and his companions walked outside into the lengthening shadows.

"What is the woman's name?" asked Juan casually.

"She is called Biburnia," he replied.

"That is a strange name," said Pedro.

"She is strange, like a two-headed chicken."

"Who is she?" asked Maromero.

"My aunt. My father's sister," said Fidel.

"Jesus," said Pedro, "no wonder they call you the destroyer. And you raped her daughter and killed her husband?"

"I was drunk," said Diamante.

Dusk built a mansion of shadows on the edge of Laredo as Bolt rode slightly ahead of Parmenter and Lupita. His clothes were soaked with sweat and stank of boiled-off salt and trail dust. His eyes slitted in the half-light of evening and his senses sparked like glittering fireflies.

He had seen the tracks, memorized them, knew

188

them well. A day old, at least, and newer now that they were at their destination.

"They'll be waiting," he said softly. "Someplace. Anywhere, from now on. You look sharp. You check your guns."

He did not look at Lupita. Parmenter looked at him and said nothing.

They knew.

Bolt knew.

It was like the world had suddenly filled with black thunderclouds and the night was coming on, and the shadows built into the hard and elusive shapes of enemies.

Bolt's gut tightened and he lifted the pistol in his holster slightly to see if it would draw free, and to give himself some comfort.

Some comfort in case all hell broke loose.

The land turned gray and featureless as they came to the outskirts of Laredo, and he knew that this was to be a showdown, the toughest showdown of his life.

He rolled his lower lip up against his upper teeth and looked at Lupita, who rode a few strides behind him.

She sat proudly tall on her dead father's black stallion, as if she were riding with his ghost. Her face was vacant with shadow, her eyes hollow holes without life.

He shuddered, cursed inwardly.

The girl looked as though she was already in hell, and a pang of regret coursed through him like a ripple of soundless thunder.

He turned his head and looked straight ahead. He drew in a deep breath, let it out slowly, and scanned the shadowy countryside, searching for shapes or movement.

They loomed up out of nowhere.

Three ghostly shadows that seemed a part of the dusk.

Shadows that suddenly burst through the dark gauze and became real.

Bolt turned his head to the side, called over his shoulder in a loud whisper.

"They're here. Spread out."

He didn't need to say more. Out of the corner of his eye, he saw Lupita lean into her horse, rein him to her left. She moved slowly, then became a shadow herself.

Parmenter rode in the opposite direction.

By then, Bolt's pistol was part of his hand, waiting.

The horsemen barreled down on them as the gray of dusk took on a darker hue.

Bolt thumbed back on his hammer, curled his finger around the trigger. Ticked off the seconds in his head, judged their speed.

They came closer and closer, and suddenly two of the riders veered off in opposite directions. The other rode straight for Bolt.

He raised his pistol, waited for the right time. The rider was almost on him when Bolt jerked the reins to the left. His horse responded instantly, throwing him out of the line of fire.

Bolt squeezed the trigger, saw the puff of white smoke. The loud boom cracked the night air, reverberated, was followed by another an instant later.

Bolt heard a brief grunt as the man toppled from his horse, thudded to the hard ground.

And then all hell broke lose. Shots rang out from all different directions. Small puffs of smoke dotted the gray gauze of dusk.

He heard a scream, much deeper than a woman's. He glanced in that direction just in time to see a man fall from his animal. Nearby, he saw Lupita on the dark stallion, a puff of smoke at the end of her extended arm. He pressed his knee into Nick's hide, turned and galloped toward her.

Two more shots rang out, one after the other.

As he rode up, he saw Lupita cringe at the sound.

And then the night became still. A thick pall of acrid smoke hung over the land.

"Are you all right?" he asked Lupita.

"Yes," she said as she lowered her arm. "Where's the doctor?"

"I don't know," Bolt said.

He whirled around when he heard the approaching hoofbeats, saw Parmenter riding toward them.

"Did you get him?" Bolt asked.

"I hit him, wounded him, but he got away."

"Which one got away?" Lupita asked.

"I don't know," Bolt said. "We'll find out."

"How can you, if he's already gone?" she asked.

"By finding out who we killed."

Bolt rode over to the closest body, the one Lupita had shot. He dismounted. The other two followed him, stayed in their saddles.

Bolt fished a match out of his shirt pocket, struck it on the fabric of his denims. He held the match over the man's face, turned to look at Lupita. She stared down at the face.

"That's Pedro," she said. "Pedro Nieves. I wish it had been Fidel. He is the one I hate the most."

Bolt mounted up, and again the others followed. He found the general area of the body, then finally found the exact spot. Again he lit a match, held it over the face.

"That one is Juan Maromero," Lupita said. "That means Fidel Diamante got away."

"How bad did you hit him?" Bolt asked.

"Superficially, I'm afraid," the doctor said. "He'll lose some blood."

Lupita's dark eyes flashed with hatred.

"We have not seen the last of him."

Chapter Eighteen

Bolt was not surprised by the small hovel where Lupita and her parents lived in Nuevo Laredo. The mestiza had told him all about it. It was one big room, not as big as the living room of the bordello. At the far end, faded curtains that hung from the ceiling separated the sleeping area from the rest of the room. The furniture was sparse. A small table, four unmatched chairs, and a worn sofa in the middle of the room. It was clean and tidy, smelled vaguely of Lupita's scent.

"Mama, I'm home," Lupita called as she walked across the room to the sleeping area. Bolt and Parmenter followed. The doctor carried his satchel.

"How are you, Mama?" Lupita said as she bent down and kissed her mother on the forehead.

Bolt could see the hurt in Lupita's eyes, the fear, when she stared down at her mother.

"Fine," her mother said, her voice not much more than a hoarse whisper. "I'm so glad you're home."

The woman was frail, with deep, hollowed-out eyes.

The flesh on her face and neck was loose, as if the woman had lost a lot of weight.

"I've brought a doctor to take care of you, Mama," Lupita said. "Dr. August Parmenter, And, this is my friend Bolt. Men, this is my mother, Alicia O'Rourke."

"Hello." Alicia's smile was thin.

Bolt nodded to the woman.

"Pleased to meet you, Alicia," Dr. Parmenter smiled. He studied the woman's appearance. The lamplight flickered across Alicia's eyes, but there was no sparkle there.

"Where's your father?" the frail woman asked as she looked beyond the others.

"Uhh, he's not here yet." Lupita said. "Do you have pain, Mama?"

"Not much. Comes and goes." She attempted a smile, fluffed at her hair with spindly fingers. "I must look just terrible, as thin as I'm getting."

"Oh, no, Mama, you're still very beautiful. I see you've got a new bed."

"Yes, Maria and Roberto brought it to me. Makes me feel like a queen."

"You are a queen, Mama. And Dr. Parmenter is going to make you feel better."

"I'd like to take a look at you, Alicia, if you don't mind," Parmenter said. He told Lupita and Tom to wait outside.

Lupita held the tears back until she and Bolt were out of the house, and then she collapsed in his arms and began sobbing.

Bolt held her tight, ran his fingers through her hair, patted her on the head, tried to comfort her.

Lupita looked up at Bolt, tears rolling down her

194

cheeks. "Oh, Bolt, Mama's so sick. She looks just awful. She's failed a lot since we've been gone."

"August will do all he can for her."

"Do you think . . ." She couldn't finish the sentence.

They sat on a weathered bench and waited. It seemed like hours before Parmenter came to the door and looked out, but it was probably only a half an hour.

"Your mother wants to see you, Lupita," he said, and he joined Bolt outside after Lupita went in.

"What's the verdict?" Bolt asked, his tone solemn.

"Not good, Bolt," the doctor said as he sat on the bench and set his satchel on the ground beside him. "She's got cancer. There's nothing anyone can do for that woman. I think she'll be dead before morning."

Bolt shook his head. "That bad."

"Yes. The growth has spread through her lymph glands, into her lungs, probably invaded her vital organs. Her skin has a yellowish cast to it. The liver is most certainly affected. She is being squeezed to death and eaten to death. It's horrible. She's in great pain, but she won't admit it. A very tough woman."

"Can you do anything for her?"

"I can give her morphia. Make her last moments more comfortable."

Bolt stood up when Lupita came out a few minutes later, drying her eyes with a kerchief.

"When can you operate on her, doctor?" she asked.

Dr. Parmenter shook his head sadly.

"But you've got to."

Bolt tried to explain to Lupita how sick her mother was, but the girl didn't want to listen.

"You don't know anything, Bolt!" she cried and

195

pounded his chest with her fists. "You and the doctor planned this. You just want the money!"

Bolt grabbed the hysterical girl by the shoulders, wanted to shake her out of her rage, but didn't. He glanced over at Parmenter.

The doctor nodded. He reached inside his bag, prepared a small dose of morphia injection. He stood up, strolled over to Lupita, and slammed the injection into the girl's arm. He walked over and stood in the doorway.

Lupita glared at Bolt, her dark eyes flashing anger. She collapsed in his arms, her legs like rubber. "You—you devil," she said. "I hate you."

"Listen, Lupita," Bolt said, "Your mother is in agony. She's dying. Let Dr. Parmenter make it easy for her."

Lupita's eyes lost their glitter when the morphia took hold. It was a small dose, meant only to calm her down.

"Your mother wants you," Dr. Parmenter said from the doorway.

Feeling oddly light, Lupita went into the house and stood beside her mother's bed.

"What the doctor says is true, Lupita. I am dying. I was just waiting for you and your father to return. The priest has been here already, given me extreme unction. Please, my daughter, let me go in peace. I can no longer bear the pain."

"I'm sorry, Mama, I didn't know."

"I am ready to go."

"I would like to sit with you for a while." Lupita turned and saw the doctor nearby. She nodded her head.

The doctor fixed another injection of the morphia,

this time much stronger. He slid it into Alicia's arm. For a few minutes he stood just beyond the curtain and watched the two women hold hands, speak softly to each other. He turned and went back out with Bolt, and the two men strolled out in the dirt yard.

Bolt fished the makings from his shirt pocket and built a smoke. He didn't smoke that much, but right now he had the craving. He offered the makings to Parmenter. The doctor took it, must have had the same need. Bolt retrieved a match from his pocket, struck it across his denims, held it out for Parmenter, then lit his own. He blew the flame out, dropped the match on the ground.

"Damned shame," Bolt said. He took a deep drag, blew the smoke up in the air, watched it for a minute until it disappeared.

"It's times like this when it's tough to be a doctor." Parmenter took a drag, released the smoke. "You see a pretty lady like that so sick and you know you can't do a damned thing about it."

"Yair. Maybe someday someone'll figure out what to do about it."

The man jumped out of the dark, sixgun blazing.

Bolt dropped the cigarette, shoved Parmenter head-first into the dirt, went for his gun. He thumbed back the hammer, aimed as he brought it up.

The Mexican ran a zigzag pattern toward them. His shots were wild.

Bolt saw his face and hated his guts.

He didn't panic. He tracked the man, waited for just the right moment.

"You coward," he shouted. "You pig. You killer of women."

Fidel Diamante stopped abruptly, took aim. His

197

eyes flashed with rage. He fired.

Too late.

Bolt held his breath before he shot. His hand was perfectly steady. He aimed between the eyes. Fired.

The bullet tore a hole in Diamante's forehead, at the bridge of his nose, ripping cartilage, spilling blood, shattering bone. His head snapped back with the impact of the blow, and an instant later, he oozed onto the ground. Dead. The moonlight splashed across the body, glistened in the pool of blood that formed around Diamante's head.

Lupita came out of the house a minute later, her shoulders sagging, her eyes damp with tears. She stared down at the dead bandit.

"It's over," she said, and took a deep breath. "My mother's gone to heaven. Fidel is on his way to hell."

Bolt gathered her in his arms, held her tight.

Parmenter glanced at the couple. "I'll go in and make out a death certificate."

Bolt nodded.

Lupita looked up at him.

"I was wrong to doubt you, Bolt," she said. "I was wrong about everything. Blind. I will go back and take my punishment."

"You won't be punished, Lupita. Just tell them where the money is hidden. I'll take care of the rest."

"And what about me?" she said as she gazed up into his eyes. "Will you take care of me? Now? Now that I need you so desperately I want to scream?"

"Yes, Lupita, I surrender."

Dr. Parmenter got a hotel room in town that night. Bolt stayed at the house with Lupita, helped her

198

with the details of her mother's death.

Later that night, after her mother's body had been removed, the funeral arrangements had been made for the following day, and the consoling neighbors had gone back to their shacks, Bolt and Lupita were alone.

"We've only got one bed, Bolt, and I just couldn't sleep in it knowing Mama died there."

"Neither could I."

"But it just isn't fair to ask you to sleep on the hard ground with nothing between us and the dirt except a couple of blankets."

"Why not?"

"Well, I'm used to sleeping on the ground. But you've got that big ranch house with all those big, soft beds. You're used to comfort." Lupita lowered her head, couldn't look at him. "All we've got is our blankets."

Bolt chucked her under the chin, tilted it up so she had to look into his eyes.

"You got me all wrong," Lupita. I've spent more nights sleepin' on the ground than you have. I prefer it. And if I've got you with me, I'll be sleepin' in a cloud anyway, so it doesn't really matter."

Lupita threw her arms around him and kissed him and he felt the need in her touch. They made love, furiously at first to vent her terrible grief. And then their lovemaking turned quiet and beautiful, as she found herself.

After the funeral the next day, Lupita and Dr. Parmenter and Bolt were saddled up and ready to go. Lupita wanted one more look at the house, and Bolt

199

followed her inside while the doctor waited for them.

"I reckon you never will tell me where that damned money's hidden," Bolt said.

"Oh, you probably would've stumbled across it some day if I hadn't lived."

"What's that supposed to mean?"

"It's buried on your property."

"My property? Where?"

"Right next to that sign that reads ROCKING BED BORDELLO."

"What? Really?"

"Yeah, if those bandits hadn't been so dumb they'd have figured it out."

"What do you mean?"

"Well, they all knew we needed that money for Mama's sickness, so they should've known we had to carry it with us back down here."

"Yair. Makes sense. Then how come you buried it at my place? You were just planning to stay the night."

"That's why. We were staying the night. Papa didn't trust those three bad ones, Diamante, Nieves, and Maromero. That's why he paid them off in San Antonio. But they knew we still had the money then. They saw it when he paid them off. He figured they'd go straight to the saloon with their pay in their hands, and he was right. Papa figured that would give us a chance to rest. So he made them think we buried the money in San Antonio. Figured that would keep them out of our hair long enough for us to get home safely with the money."

"But how come you buried it when you got to my place instead of keeping it with you?"

"You saw what happened out there that first night.

Papa didn't trust anybody. Not even the law. He wanted so much for my mother to live."

"Well, I'll be damned," Bolt grinned. "I got fifty thousand dollars buried on my land."

"That should show you I trust you, Bolt." She smiled coyly.

"What do you mean?"

"Now, you and I are the only ones in the world who know where that money is. You think I would have told you if I didn't trust you? You could get rid of me and have the money to yourself. Nobody would know the difference. Not even the law."

"You got a point there, Lupita," he grinned. "You'd better be damned sweet to me from now on."

"I plan to be, Bolt." She kissed him full on the mouth.

Lupita turned serious then, and Bolt could see the pain in her eyes when she glanced around the room.

"It's sad, isn't it, Bolt? Knowing my mother and father will never be here again. We were all so happy. I've been wondering how it would've been if my mother had lived and my father had died. I don't think Mama would have been happy without him. And if my mother had died and my father had lived, I don't think he could've stood the pain, he loved her that much."

"I know that now, Lupita. He died for her."

"But they both died so close together. It just doesn't make sense to me."

"Maybe it was supposed to happen that way."

"I think you're right, Bolt. But what about me? How can I ever live here without either one of them around?"

"Maybe you're not supposed to. You said your

father wanted you to have something better for yourself than what you had here. Maybe it's his way of saying to leave here and go out in the world and make something of yourself."

"I can see Papa laughing now." She glanced upward. "Good joke you played on me, Papa," she smiled.

"What will you do, Lupita?" Bolt asked. "Think you'll come back here and live after you straighten things out with the law?"

"I don't think so, Bolt. I don't know what I'll do."

"You'll find a way. Just don't spend your time worrying about it. Just go out and do it."

"I might take you up on your offer, Bolt," she grinned.

"What offer?"

"Massaging. You said I wouldn't have to sleep with the men who go there to get pleasured. I could do it, Bolt, if you wanted to give me a chance."

"Wouldn't work, Lupita."

"Why?"

"Because if you massaged them like you did me, you'd have to sleep with the men, anyway."

"Why?"

"You would make them so hot, you wouldn't be able to pry them away. They would want you, Lupita, just as I did."

He drew her into his arms and pressed his lips against hers.

"And if we don't get out of here right now, I'm gonna throw you back down on that blanket, you little spitfire."

"I don't think the good doctor wants to sit out in the hot sun that long."

"Neither do I."

Bolt and Lupita and the good doctor hadn't any more than ridden out of the yard when Bolt saw the strange-looking creature riding toward them.

"Who the hell is that? Well, I'll be damned if that ain't Tom."

"That's Tom?" Lupita laughed.

A minute later, Tom Penrod rode up, his body tilted at an odd angle as he rode. He had so many bandages wrapped around him, he looked like a mummy.

"I came to warn you, Bolt," Tom blurted out as he reined up on his horse.

"And who warned you?" Bolt cracked.

"Dammit, it ain't funny. Them three *bandidos* beat the daylights out of me."

Parmenter stared at the bandages a minute.

"Hmm. Professional job. Hallie do that?"

"Yeah," said Penrod, avoiding the doctor's gaze. "She fixed mè up some."

"Some?" Bolt asked. "I'd say she did a fair job with you."

"What's that supposed to mean? Hell, she wouldn't give me the time of the day."

"Never mind. We took care of the bandits."

"You mean I come all the way for nothing? I could be back in San. . . ."

"I know, Tom," said Bolt. "You could be back in San Antonio getting those bandages changed."

"Dammit, Jared, what makes you so damned smart? You act like you know it all."

Bolt didn't answer.

But Lupita did.

"Maybe he only looks smart, Tom, to one who is dumb."

Tom scratched his head a long time over that one. Bolt roared with laughter.

Bolt and Lupita and the good doctor rode away, leaving Tom to stare after them. He saw Bolt lean over, kiss Lupita on the lips. And then he saw Lupita reach for Bolt's hand.

"Well, I'll be damned," Tom said aloud. "Bolt's done tamed that spitfire, pretty as you please. Now, what's he got that I ain't got?"

TALES OF THE OLD WEST

SPIRIT WARRIOR   (1795, $2.50)
by G. Clifton Wisler
The only settler to survive the savage indian attack was a little boy. Although raised as a red man, every man was his enemy when the two worlds clashed—but he vowed no man would be his equal.

IRON HEART   (1736, $2.25)
by Walt Denver
Orphaned by an indian raid, Ben vowed he'd never rest until he'd brought death to the Arapahoes. And it wasn't long before they came to fear the rider of vengeance they called . . . Iron Heart.

WEST OF THE CIMARRON   (1681, $2.50)
by G. Clifton Wisler
Eric didn't have a chance revenging his father's death against the Dunstan gang until a stranger with a fast draw and a dark past arrived from West of the Cimarron.

HIGH LINE RIDER   (1615, $2.50)
by William A. Lucky
In Guffey Creek, you either lived by the rules made by Judge Breen and his hired guns—or you didn't live at all. So when Holly took sides against the Judge, it looked like there would be just one more body for the buzzards. But this time they were wrong.

GUNSIGHT LODE   (1497, $2.25)
by Virgil Hart
When Ned Coffee cornered Glass and Corey in a mine shaft, the last thing Glass expected was for the kid to make a play for the gold. And in a blazing three-way shootout, both Corey and Coffee would discover how lightening quick Glass was with a gun.

WHITE SQUAW
Zebra's Adult Western Series
by E.J. Hunter

Available wherever paperbacks are sold, or order direct from the Publisher. Send cover price plus 50¢ per copy for mailing and handling to Zebra Books, Dept. 1956, 475 Park Avenue South, New York, N.Y. 10016. Residents of New York, New Jersey and Pennsylvania must include sales tax. DO NOT SEND CASH.